York Tales

- whän that aprïlle

York Tales

ISBN 0-9543247-7-3

Published and distributed by
ENDpapers Ltd
Collage Corner, 2 Norman Court
YORK, YO1 7HU
ENGLAND
www.endpapers.co.uk

First edition November 2004
Second edition December 2004

Credits

Text

Editor:	Rachel Hazelwood
Copy-editor:	Elizabeth Womack
Readers:	Magdalena Chávez;
	Elizabeth Womack;
	Francesca Yeeles;
	Sally Mowbray
Prologue:	Oz Hardwick
Rat-catcher:	Andy Barker

Images

Endpapers/photography:	John Massey
Cover design:	Vince Danks and Ian Forster

Production

Design and typesetting:	Gavin Ward
Production Manager:	Sally Mowbray
Production Finance:	Francesca Yeeles

Competition Judges

Stephen Lewis	Journalist, *York Evening Press*
Kirsty Halliday	Arts and Festivals Officer, City of York Council
Dawn Simpson	Managing Director, York TV; Author
Francisco Gonzáles	Author
Katie Ireland	Author
Anna Morgan	Marketing Supervisor, Borders Bookshop, York

Contents

Introduction

This collection of short stories is the result of a competition run in 2004 by ENDpapers, a small publishing house based in York. The aim of that competition was not solely to award prizes for accomplished and distinctive writing, but to encourage submissions from unpublished and new writers; to provide them with an opportunity to showcase work that might otherwise never have been printed. However, promoting an anthology of writing by previously unheard of authors is always something of a challenge. Therefore, using a literary prize as the foundation for the book was also a means of publicising the project. Six prizes were awarded, three of which went to students from York St John College, which actively participated in the venture. I have decided not to name the winning entries. It is not my intention to devalue the competition or the stories to which prizes were awarded; but rather to recognise the merit and diverse qualities of *all* the tales chosen for inclusion.

The inspiration for the *York Tales* came from a local pest controller regaling staff at ENDpapers with a story about a Russian chef and a rat (the rat-catcher in question found that the need for his professional appraisal was made redundant by the swift action of the chef's knife). Sadly, as 'The Rat-Catcher's Tale' took place aboard a ship in Hull, it wasn't possible to include it in the volume. Nonetheless, the seed of an idea was planted for a book based on the untold stories of present-day occupations. It eventually grew into a modern day version of Chaucer's *The Canterbury Tales*, to be set in York at the beginning of the 21st century.

Why Chaucer's *Canterbury Tales*? Firstly, in the 14th century, Canterbury was England's second city. Today, after London, York has more visitors than any other city in the country and so, in terms of visitors at least, has taken up the mantle of being second in command. In addition, Chaucer and York are also linked by association with the word 'medieval'. York's undeniable appeal is its elegant juxtaposition of the ancient and the modern, a trait that is expressed in the anthology by the inclusion of a prologue written in Middle English and Chaucerian quotes at the opening of each Tale, which act as either inspiration or illustration. Secondly, as John Dryden wrote in the preface to *Fables Ancient and Modern*,

"[Chaucer] must have been a man of a most wonderful comprehensive nature, because, as it has been truly observed of him, he has taken into the compass of his *Canterbury Tales* the various manners and humours of the whole English nation in his age."

Chaucer's masterpiece paints portraits of the people of his time – a period of progress, contradiction and unrest – a time that in many ways resembled our own.

Therefore, to ensure the *York Tales* resonates with the undertones of Chaucer's creation, the writers were given explicit parameters within which to work. Each story was not only to reflect the physicality of York and its environs and be about people who live and work in or near the city; but, most importantly, the subject or theme of each Tale was to reveal an aspect of life *here and now*. One of the aims of this anthology is that someone unfamiliar with British culture, either today or in a hundred years time, should be able to read this book and get an impression of what it is, or was, like to live in York at the start of the new millennium. These contemporary signposts shouldn't simply be cultural references, but should express the social intonations of our time; provide a commentary on the values – shared or otherwise – of a cross-section of society; and explore the dilemmas, the profundity or simply the joy to be found in the human condition at the start of the 21st century.

When choosing the Tales for inclusion in the collection, I was not only looking for quality or distinctiveness; I was looking for stories which would, when viewed as a whole, be connected and contrasted – in the same way that individuals connect and contrast to create a society. We move from stories which recognise how drama can materialize out of everyday situations to modern morality tales. Another recounts a touching episode in everyday family life, told through the eyes of a child; one gives the crisis in farming a droll going-over. Sororal envy; the consequences of surrendering to lust; shameless worship of celebrity; and a macabre tale of youthful vengeance, all feature. A bar room discussion on serial infidelity sits side by side with a touching account of divine intervention and an exploration of how the past is always chasing us – even into new beginnings. A ribald and cautionary tale about the modern disease of stress is coupled with a satire on the media's often perfunctory treatment of tragedy. Tragedy is also the theme of a bold story of loss and familial exile. A further tale is a daring and moving exploration of one man's confrontation with society's increasing need to be both judge and jury; another is a timely chronicle of one woman's attempt to juggle dreams and commitments. The selection is completed with urban tales giving voice to expressions of feminism and homosexuality in the 21st century.

The variety of focus and tone, settings and themes to be found in this volume is testimony to the success of the venture. The stories range from provocative, savage and shocking to poignant, comic and grotesque. Some of the tales feature characters that are instantly familiar; some open a peephole into other peoples' lives. The subjects alternate between the momentous and the trivial, yet each narrative provides a true snapshot of contemporary life. Every short story in this collection is a social observation; each is either thought provoking, delightfully satirical or gently insightful. I hope you enjoy reading them as much as I do.

Rachel Hazelwood
York
2004

Prologue

Here Bygynneth the Book of the Tales of York

In every seson in York's faire citee

Ther longen pilgrimes al the sights to see;

The minster, castel, walls and eek the dongeon,

And maken game and chiere thurghout the toun.

They walk the way of Constantine of Rome,

The Vikings, prests and knights – and then go home.

But though York is a toun of swiche beaute

The stoones and stretes do not maken a citee.

For in these stretes ther throngen men and maydes

Who swynke and thrive CCCLXV dayes

And maken up the herte and eek the voys

Of this citee. I swere by Cristes croys,

That thurghout the world men may never see

Swich a noble or so myrie a compaignye!

The plowman, the beggere, the clerk, the wif, the cook

And many mo wol ye finde here in this booke;

Bothe the gentils and the harlots, the wynneres and wastoures,

Al grow togider and heere ben al the floures

Of hir experience and auctoritee, the sentence and solas.

So holde youre mouth and byde with me a space

For, as in Chaucer's tales of Caunterbury,

So now in the tales of York, as mote I thee,

Wil folk you telle hir moralitee and fable,

And I wil set them doun as I am able.

Certes, out of olde citees cometh tales newe,

Enditynges of divers matere and hewe.

Now I am doon, ther is namoore to seye.

Oure tales bigynne, we moot be on oure weye.

Oz Hardwick
York
2004

The Beggar's Tale

Ian Stuart

"He was the best beggere…"

The General Prologue

The cleanest town in England is Lowestoft. I've been there four times. Full of architecture. I love it. If I was ever to settle down, it would be in Lowestoft. Very clean. They have people who go round picking up matchsticks and bits of paper off the street. With tweezers. They've got special uniforms. I've seen them.

I've been a tramp eighteen years. I walk round England – that's my main occupation. I walk everywhere me. I'm proud to be a tramp and not a dosser. I hate dossers.They've got no self-respect. Now I've got self-respect. I look after myself. I've got a tie, you know, that I wear for interviews.

Give us a quid. No..go on...I haven't got nothing...I can't even afford the centre...sod off then.

I always get robbed when I come to York. Don't ask me why. It's not as though I appear affluent. Would you say I look affluent? Exactly. Dignified working class, that's what I am. When I'm working, that is. Now this that I'm going to tell you about happened last year some time, the last time I was in York, anyway, right? Some tosser of a lorry driver dropped me off at the station. It used to be good, did the station. If you were careful, you could kip down in the all-night waiting room. Warm as toast. Then the police started getting picky. Anyone who ponged a bit got chucked out. How about that for discrimination? I might have been waiting for a train and forgot to shower. I could take them to the Human Rights for that.

Anyway, it was two o'clock in the morning, or maybe four, it was bloody dark – you couldn't see your hand in front of your face – and quiet. This kid in copper's uniform chucked me out of the station. I would have knocked his lights out if I'd been twenty years younger and three inches taller, but I wasn't. So I headed down to the car park on Queen Street to find a place to settle down. Then these three lads come along. (You got kids? I got two boys. That was twenty years ago.

They'll be grown up now, I expect.) They come up to me, these lads. Baggy jeans, hooded tops and those baseball caps with the, you know, big nebs. Before I knew what was happening, two of them grabbed my arms and banged me up against the wall.

"Give us your money," they said.

"I haven't got any money!" I said. "Honest to God I haven't got any money! What would I be doing with money when it's three o'clock in the morning and no effing trains running?" The third one had this little knife in his hand – like a carpet knife – and he held it against my throat.

"Give us your money or I'll slit your throat," he said. By this time the other two were rummaging me like I was an old dressing table and they took the odd bits of coin I had about me. Then the third one – the one with the knife – kicked me in the nuts and they ran off and I was on the deck, grabbing at me balls and cursing. They just leaned against the wall, laughing.

Then I hobbled off towards the town. When I was safe away, I shouted, "Why don't you get a job?" They pulled V signs at me and one of them shouted back, "This is our job!"

I had no money. It was too late for the centre, so I stumbled down Goodramgate and ended up in a corner of Sainsbury's car park for the rest of the night. Do you know what cold is? Do you bollocks! You get beyond shivering. You hurt, inside and out, with the cold. Hurting is good. It means you're not dead yet.

I saw the sunrise. It hit the top of the Minster tower, so it was daylight up there and still night down here. Funny that.

Some woman brought me coffee in a cardboard cup. It made a good hand warmer, then I drank it. It was rush hour by this time. People moving from place to place. Cars. Purpose is a wonderful thing.

Begging is a perfectly respectable occupation. I feel no shame in being a beggar. If you go to Eastern countries, you see monks going round with begging bowls. It's religious. If I wasn't begging, then people wouldn't have the chance to give me some money, would they? Charity, that is, one of the five corporal works of mercy. Of course, when you're begging, you're not actually there. Most of you is somewhere else. Most people need a couple of cans of Special Brew, or a bit of blow, to get them off the ground, but I can do it any time I like. I think of all the places I've been, like Lowestoft, for instance.

There's a sort of alcove near St Mike's, that's the little church next to the Minster. That's a top spot because you get all the tourists coming past. I set up there; put the plastic cup out for coins, wrapped my blanket round my knees and started to play my penny whistle. When I say 'play', I don't mean, you know, like music. I can't play music for shit. I get noises out of it. It's a way of attracting attention.

Except you don't, most of the time. All you see is passing legs. Now and then a hand comes down and drops something in the cup; usually it's the brown drop, pennies and stuff.

I lost track of things a bit after that. I know I went to that burger bar on Ousegate, because I found the box on the step next to me when I woke up and there was this meaty taste still in my mouth. I'd taken a bit of blow, you see, just to relax, for recreational purposes.

The next thing I remember clearly, was looking at a pyramid. No, honest. A bloody pyramid. I thought all the pyramids were in Egypt or somewhere. I couldn't recall a pharaoh ever having been buried in York. It didn't figure in any of the history books I've read. I went into the pyramid to ask them which pharaoh was buried there, but some bloke with a badge that said "Barbican Staff" chucked me out on the street. So I was stuffed.

It was getting dark by this time, and colder. I had to start thinking about where to hole up for the night. If you're really stuck, then the centre down at Peaseholme Green will take you in – but there's lots of fighting and unruly behaviour, and you get your stuff nicked. I was thinking of trying there when I saw the church.

Churches used to be top and York has enough to let you be a bit picky. They were open most of the time, all smelling of dust and hot radiators – you could go in there for a warm. It's all different now; they shut the places up. People say it's to stop thieving and stuff. I think they don't want God to get out. A breath of fresh air might kill him. I always said a prayer when I went in a church. Haven't prayed for years. You sort of lose the knack of it, somehow.

I don't know what they call it – but you know the one – just outside Walmgate Bar. Big and black, with a spire like a skyrocket at one end. Well, I'm thinking that maybe the centre might be the best bet, but I decide to give this place a try anyway... and it's open! I push this big door and just slip inside the porch. And then I listen. Footsteps mean there's someone there, a vicar or something. Some of them will help you out, but most of them mean trouble. So I listen really hard. There's nothing, nothing at all. I notice that the warm air smells of polish.

I push this other door open that leads into the holy bit. All stained glass and carvings. Architecture. The place is packed with it. All the pews are polished and someone has put out those little cushions you kneel on; it looks as though the big gold cross at the front has had a good rub up. There's a feeling in the air...as though something is going to happen.

Now part of me is saying, "Get out quick, you don't want any trouble." But there's another part saying, "It's nice and warm here, you might as well stay for a while. Get a bit of kip." I have a look round, walking on tiptoe. The problem is the whole place is lit up like a Christmas tree – not a shady spot anywhere. Then I see this garden shed up against one wall. That's what it looks like, honest. A frigging garden shed! It's got this opening with a curtain across. I tweak the curtain back. Nobody. It's dark and warm – it'll do for me. So I nip inside, pull the curtain across and sit there in the quiet, like some mouse down its hole.

You don't know what warm is unless you've been cold. There was a heating pipe in this shed and I put my feet on it. Pure luxury! I had a few digestive biscuits in my bag and an apple, so I ate them. After a while I heard people coming in. Footsteps click-clacking on the floor, then the organ sort of cleared its throat and they were off. I didn't hear what the priest was saying, but I knew some of the hymns; 'How Great Thou Art'. I remember that from years and years ago, when I was a kid.

Now the funny thing is this: I should have been on edge, all tensed up, waiting for someone to come and chuck me out. But I wasn't. I felt better than I'd done in days. I was warm, relaxed and – you're not going to believe this – I nodded off.

I knew the second I woke up there was something different. The strip of light at the bottom of the curtain had gone, for a start. And there was the sort of silence that people leave behind them when something's happened. I tweaked the curtain back. Dark. So dark it pressed against your eyeballs.

I don't mind being alone. I pride myself on my independence. But I tell you, waking up in that lightless church scared the crap out of me. I'd lost that good feeling from earlier on. It was stifling.

After a bit my eyes got more used to it. Everything was black, but different shades of black, if you know what I mean. I could make out the windows and hear the cars going past along the Hull Road. That was a comfort. I started to feel my way back to the porch, holding my hands out in front of me, like a blind man.

It was locked. That really spooked me. I rattled the door and shouted and hollered, but no one came. It suddenly felt like being buried alive.

Then I saw this light moving around in the church. Great, I thought, there must be a caretaker and he's come to take a last look round. By this time I didn't care about anything except getting out, so I went back in.

"Hey mate!" I shouted. "Are you the caretaker?"

"You could say that," said this voice – only it came from right behind me, like he was whispering in my ear. I whipped round, tripped on the mat and fell on my arse. When I looked up....

You're not going to believe this next bit. There's no way that I can dress it up so's you'll believe me. You're going to say I was pissed, or I was flying on whiz or something. I've done that, lots of times, I know what it's like, and it wasn't like this at all.

I was looking up at an angel.

The first thing I noticed was his wings. They were bloody enormous. Eight foot at least from tip to tip, and white; so white they made a swan look mucky and you could see all the ridges in every single feather. Another thing. They were moving ever so slightly, all the time. I could feel this cool wind on my face and they made this little whiffling sort of noise.

Then I looked at him. If I was to have met him on the street I'd say he would be eighteen, maybe twenty, years old. He was black, of course, high cheekbones, big dark eyes and he had a little chinstrap beard, I recall. He was wearing a white suit. I remember that, because I thought he should have been wearing a long robe like in the Bible, and then I thought they'd have to keep up-to-date in Heaven, just like anywhere else.

"What do you really want, Neville?" he said.

Now that floored me. No one calls me Neville. Haven't done for years. I'm Nev or Never Never Man, but not Neville. Ever.

The last person to call me Neville was my mum and she's dead.

"I want…I want…."

Then a crafty thought struck me. If he was real, then he'd know what I want without me saying. That's the whole point of angels and saints and stuff, isn't it? They got the knowledge. They *know*.

"You know," I said, "You know what I want…"

He held out his hand towards me. His skin was the same colour as copper beech leaves; his fingers were long and thin. I felt his hand on my head.

The next thing I knew, I was on my knees in the gutter outside the Wagon and Horses, looking up at the outside of the city walls. How I got out of that church I'll never know. The rain was sluicing down the back of my neck and the traffic roaring past showered me with the dirty water off the street.

"Disgusting!" someone said, and I heard a woman's heels click away into the dark.

I got to my feet and checked to see if everything was working. No aches. No pains. I tried to work out how I'd got out of the church. No answer. I rummaged in my bag to make sure all my stuff was there. Then I put my hand in my back pocket. Paper. A thin wad of paper. I pulled it out…

Fifty quid. Five tenners. Now that was clever. Anyone like me with a fifty quid note in his hand was distinctly suss, but a tenner at a time – that was believable. I tried to think if anyone had given me fifty quid during the day. It wasn't possible. And I knew I hadn't nicked it. I knew that. It could only have been *him*.

First thing I did was to go to the chippy on Layerthorpe and get one of each and a mug of tea. I sat inside, enjoying the steamy warmth until closing time. You might think it was all some kind of dream, but the more I thought about it, the more real it was in my mind. Now dreams don't do that, do they? They just fade away. After an hour or so I'd made my mind up. It was time to move on, so I headed up to that big roundabout on Hull Road.

As a rule you have to wait for hours before you get a lift these days. People think you're a paedophile or something. But this time I hadn't been there for more than five minutes, when this big truck pulled in to the side of the road.

"Want a lift mate?" said the driver.

"Where are you going?"

"Lowestoft."

"That'll do me," I said.

The Story-Teller's Tale

Helen Sant

"But yet I praye to al this compaignye,

If that I speke after my fantasye,

As taketh not agrief of that I seye;

For myn entente nys nat but for to pleye."

The Wife of Bath's Prologue

In ancient time, the story-teller was a raggedy Romany, with dust-travel hair and animal skins for clothes. In the Middle Ages she was a minstrel, disguised as a boy, hair cropped, gaudy hose stockings and carrying a battered lute. A female minstrel was unusual – but not impossible.

In the new millennium in the City of York, you can find a story-teller on many a corner, some with presence, some without. Sometimes you only need the cheek of the devil and a box of paints to tell your story. The musicians, the mimers, the costumed employees of historical attractions, the pavement artist and the tour guide, all pass through Stonegate, with its blend of modern commercialism and ancient history. From behind glass-fronted doors, cream confectionery tempts and teddy bears beckon; a rainbow of candles catches the eye and aromatic herbs entice. A snickleway known as Coffee Yard, off the main street, is where seventeenth century printers drank and gossiped away their long day's work. The ghostly echoes of their conversations are buried under twenty-first century hustle and bustle. This is one of the stops on the tour. Eve is the modern-day story-teller of the most traditional kind. If she doesn't know the history, she just adds fiction, like the time she fooled visitors about the little stone devil above the entrance to the snickleway.

"He's a reminder to the citizens of York to lead a sinless life," she says. He is no such thing. The small red-and-black statue is a statement that Stonegate used to be a place of printers, their 'devils' being another name for their apprentices – those they could blame for their mistakes. Eve tells the crowd that the ornamental devil may be linked to the tale of Joseph Marbury, whose mother prayed to Lucifer for his recovery from illness as a child and who unwittingly cursed him in the process. She died in his place and the adult Joseph could not live with the guilt.

"So be careful what you wish for because someone,

somewhere, will have to live with the consequences," says she. Her audience receives this message with mixed feelings. Some doubt, some smile and some shiver inside where no one sees. Fiction is always better than truth, the story-teller muses.

Fiction is better than truth, because the life of this modern-day-story-teller is dull in comparison to the life of her stories, collectively a wild, breathing, colourful creature. Joseph Marbury is stuck in his world of torment – unable to decide his own fate, motionless as an artist playing a living statue – for he is a character of Eve's imagination. Since he does not exist, he is compelled to dance to any tune she plays, just so long as Eve's boss doesn't find out. The manager of the tour company is an unforgiving man of little imagination and large belly, which he fills with rich food and even richer drink. If he caught Eve making up stories for the tourists, she might be in trouble for not telling history like it is. She has to be careful. This is a girl who tries to cut corners, to go the back-door way – she was once given the sack for making a joke about Vikings to tourists, on the grounds that she might give offence to Scandinavian visitors.

When Eve arrives home, her lover, Jack, makes her a cup of tea. She prefers to think of him as a lover. It sounds much more fun than a boyfriend. All is secure. In the twenty-first century, there are no dragons lurking in corners, no wild spirits waiting to rise out of the attic and float into the living room, upsetting the careful arrangement of the Ikea coffee tables. There are no demons to tame. Or are there?

Eve feels her world is colourless and, if she knew who some of her ancestors were, she might think their lives exciting, compared to hers. Stepping into ancient time, you can find Eve's ancestor of the animal skins, with a husband *and* a lover, a campfire for solace and river water for refreshment. In comparison, the medieval minstrel has no man to call her own, since she is used to wandering and never settling.

The Romany takes off the battered cowhides from her footsore feet and watches a red sun sinking beyond still waters. What need has she for excitement when her arms are bloody and scratched from battles? She longs only for peace, lulling sweet children to slumber with song and winning approval from the grandmothers with her tales of heroism – these are the things that make her happy. Feeling the lick of inviting orange fire at the night-time gatherings; waiting for word from the warrior, whose arms have strangled many an enemy and also entwined around her waist in violent love. Serving her gentler husband a stew of woodland treasures gathered that morning, whilst nursing the babe in her cradle – these are the things that matter; not war, not bloodshed, not quarrels of meaninglessness. A village woman must know her priorities. To be a fighter is all well and fine, but time for rest must come. There must always be time for story-telling and reflection.

The minstrel is eating a piece of undercooked chicken at the table of a very hospitable gentleman. They laugh and catch each other's eye. He knows she is no boy beneath that gaudy garb, but he won't tell.

Away from York's tales of crooks, hauntings and curiosities, Eve sat opposite Jack at the end of the working day, both eating chicken and microwaved vegetables. She had given up looking for telltale signs of a scuffle in the stationery cupboard with a bottle-blonde wanton of diminished responsibility, knowing that Jack would never cheat. She sighed, recalling a man she had once known biblically. As her boyfriend, he had never been faithful. He had brought her flowers and inventive tales, and, inevitably, heartache. She didn't miss the pain, but she missed the passion. Jack caught her eye, "You know, I lost my job today."

"What? You lost… What's happened?"

"It's all very sudden, but the whole place is closing. Graham called me into his office today. Gave me the news. At least I'll get a generous redundancy. Not like the workers on the factory line."

"Oh." A slight pause. "No more free chocolates then," she murmured, with genuine regret.

"I guess not, but then you know what some of the workers put into the sweets on the production line."

"Oh, don't remind me when I'm eating. So, what will you do? Were there any managerial positions in the paper tonight?"

"I had a quick scan in the Evening Press. Couldn't see any. I might join you giving tours of York. Or I could busk. Maybe I could play the flute."

"Well," she said, between chicken pieces, "the penny whistle is supposed to be easy. Only a few notes to learn." She fondly remembered the man begging at Bootham Bar, one of the city's ancient stone gateways. With a trill on his instrument, he received her donation and shrugging, he told her he couldn't really play. Yet another story-teller.

"Perhaps I could become a gentleman thief," said Jack.

"I hardly think so!" Jack looked hurt by the obvious scorn in her tone.

"Why not?" he said quietly. Then much more quietly, "Actually, I already am."

"What do you mean? Returning stuff to shops that isn't really from there, doesn't count, you know." Jack put his fork down in the gravy, more slowly than a knight of old would have thrown down his gauntlet, but with just as much theatrical dignity.

"I am. But it's only ever been a sideline. I've always wanted to tell you."

Eve struggled to take in this confession with greater difficulty than with the previous news of job loss. She rubbed her cheek for a while, and then her chin, as if trying to wipe off excess foundation; playing for time whilst she assessed Jack's sanity levels.

"What are you talking about Jack? Are you trying to tell me that you're a modern-day Turpin?"

"No, not really. You've told me enough times, Turpin was a cheap thug and not really a gentleman highwayman."

"Right." She still wasn't sure of his sanity. Jack went on to tell her about the teenage shoplifting: a tie pin here, a box of aftershave there, only quality stuff. It had started as a hobby and had developed into a habit in adult life to avoid paying for over-priced goods. It was, Jack maintained, a kind of Marxist statement in a capitalist system. He had acquired jewellery, gourmet food and was planning on hitting a lingerie shop for a negligee for Eve that would stir the blood of a seasick Viking. Eve was horrified; the chicken grew colder between them.

"So you're a kleptomaniac!"

"Eve, please! Don't be melodramatic. I consider myself a gentleman thief. I have a code of honour, of course. I never steal from individuals."

"Well all the same – it's dishonest. How much of the stuff you've 'bought' me over the years is actually stolen?" He discovered a bone in his mouthful of chicken, just at that moment, and whilst he dealt with this, the question went unanswered.

"You know," he resumed, "I thought you always wanted me to be more exciting. Besides, I never get caught, so you needn't worry about that. It's just a little game really."

"This is the craziest conversation. Jack, you must stop. It's not as if you need to steal, even without a job now. You'll soon find something. Don't you see? You have got to stop this... *game* as you call it." Jack just looked at her, took her hand and kissed it gallantly like the most sensual of rogues.

"I can't," he whispered.

The Romany did not complain when her lover stole. He found wonderful trinkets in the spoils of battle; amulets taken from dead men's necks, blood-spattered, mud dulling the shine. He'd clean them up and bring them to her.

The minstrel girl stole bread from market stalls if really hungry. She spent most of her time in the company of thieves, rogues and men on the edge of life.

"Lucy Is Having A Party" was the message in the morning post. Eve eyed the invitation with a mixture of pleasure and relief. Since Jack's confession the previous evening, she had begun to worry; the rattle at the letterbox had made her jump. Still, the police did not normally send postal arrests. Jack was sprawled across the sofa, reading yesterday's paper, still in his dressing gown.

"Lucy is having a party," Eve told him. "It's her house-warming."

"Great. When is it?"

"Two weeks Saturday." He mumbled something.

"What are you going to do today?" she said more sharply.

"What? Oh, I'm going to the job centre later."

"Oh, right. I'll come with you," she said. "It's my day off."

"You don't need to do that."

"Of course I do. I want to give you moral support." That and make sure he didn't do a detour to some high street store to loot something valuable. She wanted to ask him how he managed to get the stuff out of the shop without alarms going off, but she thought better of it.

Two and a half weeks later, they stood in the hallway of Lucy's new house. The music was loud; there were too many people, most of whom she had never seen before, and the chilli had all been eaten. Lucy greeted them with all the enthusiasm of a girl who had been knocking back the Beaujolais. They had barely had time to catch up with one another, when their hostess was called away by a man in a brightly coloured shirt, which should have been condemned.

The past slice of Eve's life had been stressful. She had barely let Jack out of her sight. She was constantly wondering if his secret had been discovered. Her dreams were troubled, but her bedtimes were luscious. The charms of a gentleman thief were a novelty compared to those of an ordinary man. Being mistress to a criminal had its compensations, she thought. Then an incident unfolded in a cruel twist of fate that was to change her mind.

The party was almost over. The last few stragglers were vying for sleeping space on the floor, or ringing for taxis. Eve was pleasantly tipsy on a sagging floor cushion, when Lucy came hurtling into the room.

"I can't find my necklace anywhere," she said a little tearfully. "I put it down on the dressing table. I know I did. And it's gone!" People began to ask questions. What did it look like? Could she have been mistaken? When did she last see it? Eve, however, asked no questions, but instead eyed Jack across the room, as he stood next to the mantelpiece, as if posing for a family portrait. He felt her glare, as withering as that of the most carnal of creatures poised to attack and devour. The intensity of her wrath was just simmering, when a suddenly sobered-up Lucy let forth an exclamation of joy. The man with the loud shirt had produced the missing necklace, from

Droopy's basket. (Droopy was a slobbering spaniel, who thought he was a magpie and who sometimes made off with small possessions of Lucy's.)

The drama over and the risk of suspicion lifted from those guests she didn't really know that well, Lucy relaxed. Eve dropped her stone-turning gaze from Jack and announced they had better be going. As the door closed on their smiles, the argument began on the first crunch of path gravel.

"Thanks for the vote of confidence. You thought I'd taken her necklace!" he began.

"Well, what do you expect? Naturally, it seemed as if…"

"You thought I'd steal from a friend?"

"Well, why not? I don't know how it works. A thief is a thief."

"I told you I have a moral code," he hissed.

"Moral code? Theft is theft. It's all the same to me." Jack stopped at the corner of street. He lowered his voice, aware of a silhouette at a nearby window.

"Eve. I'm not a thief."

"Right. Well, whatever name you give it…"

"No. I'm not a thief. I made it up."

"You did what?" She wanted to pick up a paving stone and hurl it at him.

"I made it up. I thought it would make me seem more exciting. I just did it – I don't really know why, but I did."

"You mean I've been watching you for the past fortnight to keep an eye on you, and dreading the ring of the phone, because you're a *liar*?"

"Well a liar's not as bad as a thief, is it? Eve, how could I be a thief? How do you think I could get the stuff out of the stores without alarms going off?"

"I don't know! Why did you lie to me?"

"Because things were going stale between us. I thought you were bored with me."

"I suppose I was, but that's no reason to go telling me lies. What else have you been lying about?"

"Nothing else." He hung his head. "You're the story-teller. You like imagination, don't you?"

Eve was unsure how to continue this story. She could go back to the arms of this familiar figure, with an embrace and a kiss to mend the harsh quarrel, or she could leave him, exchange his familiarity for the single life. It was her story; one of a relationship frayed a little at the edges and a lover who had felt unloved enough to try some creative embroidery.

"Is it true about the job?" she asked.

"Of course *that's* true. Eve, I'm sorry, but deep down you want someone dangerous. Well, I'm afraid you've got me."

"Deep down a lot of women want someone dangerous. And a lot of men want someone dangerous too. There's nothing wrong with you, sweetheart. Nothing at all. I'm sorry." She kissed him, and the silhouette at the window took the form of a monster-woman with bad hair. She leaned out to shout for her cat and disturbed a wonderful romantic moment. Eve and Jack laughed. Real life is, after all, just that – real. Her words come back to her. "Be careful what you wish for." This is the man she will probably marry. He is honest, not a philanderer, not a real rogue, but he is able to step into a fantasy if he chooses.

The Romany wanders into the forest. It is early morning. The night rain has left fresh caresses on the bark of trees and the scattered earth. Its perfume is just a promise of spring, innocent and intoxicating, like blossom. Under her feet, she feels the textures of green brackish stones and fertile soil, alternately rough and soft. In the middle of this haven, the warrior used to meet her, but not any more. By the well on the very edge of the village, they would make their secret plans and the last time they were there she showed him a necklace, but only because he admired it.

"It's beautiful, like you," he said, grabbing at the bone carved symbol – a runic protector. She looked at him steadily.

"My husband gave it to me. He made it for me," she said. The warrior knew then that she would never be his. He knew that she loved her husband again and that his time in her life, as a lover, was over. He had lost the contest.

"Good things come to those who wait," says the minstrel girl, in mischievous satisfaction. His words had been handsome, crowned with the treasure-touch of his flirtatious fingers. Could any red-blooded damsel have resisted such a man? Having succumbed to his advances, she had found him most enjoyable. Now she laces up her tunic and rolls off the blankets. Running to the window, she gazes out onto the street below, to see the procession.

The lad, Geoffrey, still lazing upon the floor, watches her. For a moment, he almost loves her. A muse can have strange effect upon a man. This one will live in his imagination, long after their encounter. She is worth writing about, being a creature of infinite earthiness, hailing from Bath – a pretty place to come from. She could one day be the voice of women in his tales. He might paint her as having had five husbands. Why not? All stories are but sweet deceits woven on life's loom. Master Chaucer sighs at the poetical form of such a comely wench. Yes, one day when he writes his tales, his little conquest will be in there somewhere.

The Carriage Worker's Tale

David Darton

"To chirche was myn housbonde born a-morwe

With neighebores, that for hym maden sorwe…"

The Wife of Bath's Prologue

As I was setting out, I found the Dictaphone, accidentally included in the stuff I packed up when I cleared my desk yesterday and left the firm for the last time. I didn't use it much for my job, as I could never organize my thoughts sufficiently for a business report without seeing it in writing. But spying it just before leaving the flat, I suddenly felt an urge to record this journey. For me? For prosperity? I'm not sure. I remember in a first-year psychology course being told that older people often do something like writing their memoirs, or painting, in order to leave their mark on the world when they have gone.

Oh dear, sorry about that long, spluttering pause. I should have turned the machine off for a moment. I had better apologise in advance to whoever is listening to this and trying to transcribe it. Apart from the likelihood of it being muddled, I'm feeling particularly unwell today and coughing quite a bit as I speak. Perhaps it is the emotional stress and uncertainty that I know the end of today's journey is going to bring.

Well, it's an hour later and we are just approaching York, the city I grew up in. I guess this will be the last time I need to visit it. An old lady who got on at Huddersfield took a liking to me. She chatted non-stop to Leeds, hence the pause in my narrative. I heard her say to the person who met her off the train what a nice, young man I was. If I am honest and immodest, I guess that I agree. I *am* a nice young man. It's good to like yourself when you need the strength to tackle the difficulties I have ahead.

I hadn't planned to, but I have just walked up from the station to the centre of the city, although my destination lies in the opposite direction. Delaying tactics, I guess. I have always been good at that.

It is really industrial York that has imprinted this city on my soul, rather than the olde world, historical city that I am gazing on now. But I love all of this city of my birth: the hidden, hard parts that lie behind the tourist façade, as well as that which the tourists see. I should have come back sooner, really. One of the few things I regret in my life is feeling unable to do so for so long. But maybe the time was necessary in order to come to terms with everything. Now I am back and things have moved in a full circle. I feel content about that and ready for what comes next, although today is not going to be easy. I haven't spoken to her in so long.

I see that the city has changed since I have been away. Coffee houses are everywhere, the street buskers seem more sophisticated and the shops more expensive. Internet cafes abound. There is a whole, new village within the city, the Latin Quarter in which I am sitting now. Over time these new communities will be threads in the city's cultural tapestry. But only threads. The Dickensian streets remain the same. The pubs and other haunts of my misspent youth that I passed are all still here.

Above all, York is rooted in its history. Its prosperity rises and falls, but always comes back. Some places seem to have an energy that allows them to re-invent themselves to suit the economic or political requirements of the day. York is such a place of energy. Those people who encapsulate old values and traditions seem to combine with the constant flow of incomers in creativity rather than in conflict. But there are two histories in recent years and mine is the one that does not appear in the guidebooks, though they are linked by death. I really feel, you know, that death is something we have to re-learn how to embrace. Otherwise it is just tragedy and a waste. I won't allow it just to be that.

I passed the tourist office on the way up here and, out of idle curiosity at what the marketers have to say about the place, I picked up a couple of leaflets. They remind me that the official, approved history of York is spectacular. No wonder it is one of the most visited cities in the country. This leaflet proudly announces that York is Britain's oldest capital city, pre-dating London by a significant period. It was prominent in Roman times as Eboracum – indeed the emperor Constantine was 'crowned' here. In medieval times, York's importance rose again, with the Minster as the architectural crowning glory of this period. The energy involved over several generations to complete, it still inspires me, even though I have seen it on the horizon all my life.

Perhaps the most unique part of the city's tourist attraction, however, is its even older connection to the Vikings, given much more space in these brochures than the Roman heritage. The Vikings have left their impression in numerous ways. I still get a childhood kick that the York word for street is 'gate', while the word for the city gates that surround the city is 'bar'. But what the Vikings were best known for was their bloodthirsty approach to life and the death that seemed to surround them. This is really their biggest attraction.

York has always had its share of scandalous connections, but ones that seem connected to death rather than sex and money. There was the massacre of hundreds of Jews in Clifford's Tower. Dick Turpin was sentenced, imprisoned, hanged and buried in York. Guy Fawkes went to school here and I remember that no one at St. Peter's, where he was a pupil, could burn an effigy of Guy on Guy Fawkes night, as happens across the rest of the country. And, I think, there is still a by-law that says one is allowed to kill approaching Scotsmen from the city walls. Death, of course, also plays its part in making York the most haunted city in the Kingdom.

I think the connection with death is healthy. Too few of us these days are really conscious of our mortality. Death needs to be de-sanitised, because awareness of it gives us the energy to live our lives to the full and appreciate each moment.

It is death of a recent time, not yet developed into any romanticized ghost story, that is the reason for my long absence from York and my return now. Death that has affected a very small part of the city, important in its recent history, but now finally, after some fits and starts, gone forever.

I must not delay my return to that part of the city any more, or it will get so late that I will have to postpone things until tomorrow. If I do that, my resolve may falter and I have to speak to my mother. At least I have to try. It is strange how you cannot escape the need for parental approval. How you need them to say the words of absolution that mean they are still there for you.

I couldn't actually help delaying things a bit more and went back to the station via an old haunt of mine. The drink I had there brought back memories that were all good, despite my mixed feelings today. Back at the station I turned in the opposite direction to the tourists and, after only a couple of minutes, was on the desolate footbridge over countless railway sidings that brings me to a place that overlooks a focal point of my youth, the carriage works. Not that most of us who populated it would recognize it now. The old building is still there. But it is an empty shell now, without the noise and bustle, the steam and clanging of metal on metal that you would once hear from here. Next to it, I can see a recent development of shiny new houses, put up since I left, but as tightly squashed together as the tiny terraces that I grew up in just further down the road.

My parents lived there since before I was born. It was a close community of traditional working-class values and most of us, father and son, were employed at the carriage works. It was one of the major employers of the local economy.

I have walked up towards my home. As I look at the area now it seems slightly forlorn with the streets dominated by greys and dull browns. My rose-tinted memory of life here is not, however, of grey and bleakness. It is one of colour. We were poor; we were not very mobile and everything we did – work, school, football, shopping, socializing at the working-men's club – was with the same people. We knew almost everything about each other and guessed the rest, all of which was a potential scandal and something to feel superior about. That was the colour of my life; the local never-ending soap opera that lit up the dull grey streets, the boring, unhealthy food and the tedious work.

Of course, the soap opera wasn't 'never-ending'. Times change. I escaped – though not soon enough – to a life of broader horizons, which my low-aspiration school – closed now – and my holiday jobs, at the carriage works of course, never really prepared me for. Around me, my close-knit community had begun to erode anyway. I doubt I will find many I know now, even though my mother still lives here. Building trains, one of the mainstays of the local economy that you assumed would last forever in this railway-junction city, began a slow, painful decline well before I left. Now tourism, retailing, insurance, the university and the just-surviving chocolate factories dominate the local economy. The heavy industry is largely gone.

But why did it have to take my dad and so many more of us with it?

Well, there's the house. The net curtains are still the same, though not twitching. I'm still hesitating. The last two times I telephoned, she hung up as soon as she heard my voice. I guess I had better explain. Another delaying tactic, no doubt, and dusk is already with us.

In a sense, it began with my dad's end. It's strange how, even after just five years, the memories of someone you loved fade and merge into a chaotic set of images that it is difficult to connect chronologically. How sometimes you are not even sure if you can remember his face properly. I have to keep checking the single photo I have of him. Not that I want to remember his face as it ended, racked in pain. If only I had acted earlier.

The moments of my dad that I remember most fondly are, ironically, those that have come back to haunt me and finally to shape my life. My dad, Stephen – Steve to his friends – had always been a traditional father. A man of few words, whose leisure pursuits were those of the men around him – mainly football, drinking at the working-men's club; later on, playing bowls. He was a man of few words and scathing of anyone who did not fit into our idea of what 'normal' was. Steve found being a father difficult; society, at least that part of it that surrounded us, had not prepared him for any caring role or for what is nowadays termed 'quality time with the children'. Emotional expression, outside the football terraces and the odd flash of extreme anger at home, was not on the menu. And if society didn't prepare him, he didn't prepare me. I never was able to tell him I loved him during those last, painful days. Though at the very end he must have known.

But I digress. My fondest memories were when I ceased to be a child in his eyes and became instead a 'son to be proud of' among his peers. Like during the holidays, in my late teens, when, working at the carriage works, I would sit in the dusty old store room, eating my sandwiches with him and his mates, listening to their banter as one of the lads. Or him taking me into the club for a drink and telling me how proud he was that I had turned out 'alright'.

Dad was shorter than I am now. That much I remember

well. Stocky and dark with a round face, but a good, full head of hair. And fit. So it took a while for us to recognize how ill he was. We knew it was a possibility, of course. A number had died already. But it was a bit of a lottery and one that you never really allowed yourself to believe you would lose. He probably knew sooner than we did, but, like I said, he was never good at emotional stuff and did not know how to tell us.

When it came to a head, I was at the sixth form college, much to everyone's surprise, studying 'A' levels. Some unknown quirk of the genes had made study and good exam results come easily. But I still felt more at home down the club or in a pub, than in the new trendy bars most of my class mates were frequenting.

The way we were treated at the end, though, changed all that and I couldn't wait to escape to university. I was not going to be powerless for the rest of my life.

Mum and dad had been to Belgium on one of those 'booze cruises'. Two nights on the night-crossing from Hull and a day in-between shopping at Zeebrugge's hypermarket, with a couple of hours in nearby historic Brugge thrown in. They hadn't got back when I left for college that morning, but I was looking forward to hearing about their trip – they were always hilarious in their scathing accounts of the other passengers and our fellow Europeans across the sea.

When I returned, they weren't in. Instead there was a note from my mum. Oddly it instructed me to call the vicar.

My mum was the only one of us who had any religious leanings. I had stopped going to church as soon as I was old enough to insist. My dad had never come with the two of us.

A new, young vicar turned up at the door half-an-hour later. He didn't waste words. "Your dad has been taken poorly on the way back from Belgium. They're at the District hospital." He hesitated.

My world seemed to lurch sideways and a dread that had always been there rose to the surface. I looked at the vicar, struggling for words.

"It's alright," I said. "It's Asbestosis, isn't it?"

"Yes. Your mum didn't want to tell you over the phone or in public at the hospital." Hence the vicar. It wouldn't have been my choice, but he was doing his best.

"It's terrible. You know this is the sixth one I've been involved in."

Six or a hundred, it was no longer about abstract statistics. Actually, my dad was about number twenty-five in the mounting death toll. There were already ten fatherless families in the area that I knew about.

Asbestosis crept up on you. It would finally kill a man some years after the damage was done – sometimes just a couple of years, sometimes many more. When my dad was diagnosed, it was still only talked about in hushed tones, but anger was mounting. The carriage works was already closed, but the company still existed in some form.

"You know, the company isn't accepting any responsibility," my father said angrily, when his best mate from his school days succumbed. But evidence was mounting. The company began to put aside some funds for potential compensation claims. And the Union was putting the widows in touch with lawyers who would take their cases. I had only half listened. After all, these things only happen to the person next to you. Not to you. It's how they send soldiers over the front line. But perhaps my father's anger was because he knew. At least knew the odds weren't that good.

My dad was phlegmatic, as usual. He had no religion, but did not seem phased by his fate. "People like us," he said, on one of the rare occasions that we talked around the edge of his impending death, "live life for ourselves and those around us. I've done it as well as I could and you – you're clever – and will do it even better."

My mum held up well too. For his – and maybe my – sake. The only outward sign was more trips to church than before.

Until the funeral itself, the only one who cried in front of me was a tough fifty-year old. The District Commissioner of the Scouts Association. My dad had been a Scout leader and representative on numerous national bodies for years. "We're going to miss him," he said, "You probably don't realize how much he contributed, but we agreed last night that we would create an annual award for special achievement to be presented in his honour each year. Perhaps you and your mum could come and present it?" It was then that he broke down. I didn't know what to do. Well, an eighteen-year old shouldn't have to handle all that.

As things turned out, I never did get to go to any of the presentations. But I heard from others that my mum did it with much dignity.

Perhaps it was a mercy that my dad went fairly quickly. He was only at home for about two months after that first visit to the District, before he had to be admitted permanently. Strangely, I coped by escaping into my study and my marks actually went up. But I couldn't escape the physical strain that began to dent even my dad's philosophical attitude. The struggle to breathe became more and more pronounced and his digestive system was racked by pain. He could no longer disguise the agony that swept in waves through his body at ever-increasing intervals.

I can almost rationalize the death of the carriage works, the death of the community and even the individual endings as part of the declines that are necessary to the constant re-invention of the city. But only almost. When my dad was hospitalized for the last painful, lingering six weeks of his life, it was a personal tragedy. One that I could not bear.

It was also a tragedy for York. They may have been the worker bees, but most of the men who died contributed much more. They were the volunteers for the Scouts and Cubs. They were the people who turned out on wet Sunday mornings to enable young people to play soccer. They were the people who drove the elderly to the shops or organized the fund-raising for the local children's hospice. Maybe death is necessary for renewal. But York would have been better off if these men had lived. And the city has never really acknowledged this tragedy or valued the lives that were lost. It doesn't contribute to the image, like the Viking deaths do.

And that's when I got angry. Angry at my dad's acute pain that no one seemed able to stop. But also angry at the lack of value given to my dad's life and our powerlessness to do anything about it.

The company finally accepted some responsibility for the asbestos dust flying around parts of the carriage works. But then they haggled over every last penny of compensation. After my dad's funeral, there was no closure. My mother had to tell the story of my dad's life and death countless times: to friendly lawyers; to unfriendly ones. And we were never told what was going on; I had to pester even our own lawyers for any information.

The only thing they seemed interested in valuing was what his lifetime earnings might have been if he had lived. No one acknowledged the other contributions of my dad's life. And no one seemed at all sensitive to our grief, except at the level of platitudes and the offer of a cup of tea when we had been left waiting in an outer office for hours, while more pressing matters that had come up were dealt with.

Then, after one particularly distressing meeting, I finally broke down and told my mother what I had done.

At first, when my dad went into hospital, the pain was largely controlled. I was fascinated by all the equipment. Partly to engage my dad and break the monotony of the bedside hours, we discussed with the nurses all the details of the monitoring and drips and so on. I wanted him to feel that it was not something destroying his dignity; that it was something okay to talk about.

But then the pain got more acute. Dad floated in and out of consciousness and only sometimes knew who I was. He seemed to be in a constant state of pain whatever his state of consciousness. But his body was strong and fit and fighting every inch of the way. At times his eyes seemed to be pleading with me. Finally, I realized that I was not powerless; that I had the knowledge to end the suffering. After all, what purpose was it serving?

There was a moment of lucidity. My mum and my gran were having a break down at the cafeteria. I asked him. He couldn't really speak. But I knew. He looked directly and firmly into my eyes for the first time in days. And we knew, despite the lack of words, how much we loved each other. I held his gaze as I turned the valve to 'maximum'. As his eyes began to lose focus, he smiled for the first time in a couple of weeks. Shaking, I turned the valve back again.

But it was against the law of God. My mum hasn't spoken to me since I told her. I've tried several times, but she doesn't want to know.

That just has to change. I have to knock on that door. We have to make things right. As you have no doubt realized as I have coughed and spluttered my way through this, I don't have long left. Those school holiday jobs at the carriage works. And especially the packed lunches in that dusty storeroom with my dad and his mates. The times that had meant so much to me growing up have layered my lungs with asbestos dust.

I resent, rather than fear, the fact that I am going to be dead soon. There was so much I wanted to do. But the least I can do is not to leave this world without resolving things with mum. And there is something I do fear. The pain. I have never been very good at that. And the only person who could love me enough to turn the valve for me, would be my mum. If I can persuade her that her religion should allow that mercy.

The door-knocker seems so much heavier than it used to…

The people and specific events in this story are fictitious. But it is dedicated to the seventy-plus people who have died, without fanfare, so far, from Asbestosis caught at the York carriage works. In particular, it is dedicated to Trevor Lea, who I only knew posthumously through his family and in particular his son, Colin. Like Stephen in the story, and like many of those who have died, Trevor was brave and resigned to his fate, largely without bitterness. And, also like many of the others, he made real and lasting contributions to his community and those he knew. He is sorely missed.

The Graduate's Tale

Annette Oliver

"That I am dronke, I knowe it by my soun;

And therfore if that I mysspeke or seye,

Wyte it the ale of Southwerk, I you preye."

The Miller's Prologue

37

Sam, the new, fresh-faced graduate trainee and most recent member of the circle, had joined the group of friends from the transport depot who were all having a drink in The Blue Bell, on Fossgate, with some of the locals. He had arrived halfway through a heated debate and, having led a fairly sheltered middle-class life, was slightly wrong-footed at the scene being played out before him. Tom, the battle hardened, but highly respected transport manager of a small York delivery company, was red-faced with indignation and disbelief. He was fairly spitting out his words, along with a beery spume.

"…but Leicester!" he heard Tom exclaim in abject disbelief. "Why on earth Leicester?"

"Got a good rugby team," Sam (who, incidentally, had been quite a useful fly half in his college days) offered as his contribution to a conversation he knew nothing about.

A heavy silence descended. All eyes turned to Sam, who blushed a little under the oppressive glare. "What on God's earth, has rugby got to do with it?" bellowed the landlord.

"Well, he might have a point," ventured Joe. "Both involve a lot of rucking and mauling."

Sam half smiled as the light slowly began to dawn. "Would this be a good time to ask what's happened?" he ventured hesitantly.

"It's our Dave," replied Joe, "only gone and buggered off to Leicester with another woman."

Joe, who worked on a nearby farm, was not noted for his quick wits, but he demanded a key role in the tale about to unfold, as he was in some distant way related to the errant errand man Dave.

Dave had been given the task of showing Sam the 'practical' side of the business, and so they had spent many jovial hours together, passing the time of day but not passing the transport cafés. Dave had said these stops were a vital part of broadening Sam's education. During this time Dave had also dwelt long and hard on his home life with 'his lass', thus broadening Sam's education even further.

"No, I can't believe it! I thought he was happy with his lass," gasped Sam incredulously.

"He was happy with a lot of people's lasses!" grimaced Joe. "Not a great fan of mahogany, our Dave."

"Monogamy," corrected Sam.

"Aye. That an' all lad, that an' all," said Joe, seemingly oblivious to the correction.

"Well, he's always been one for believing there are plenty of fish in the sea," Tom interjected, helpfully.

"And he's hooked more than a few old trout in his time," chuckled Joe, "but to up sticks and leave and then, to cap it all, to go to bloody Leicester."

"It'll be the right-turns." It was Nigel who spoke. This caused double consternation; firstly what did right-turns have to do with extra-curricular activity and, secondly, what was the semi-recluse Nigel doing in the pub at all? Most perplexing.

But first things first.

"Right-turns?" enquired Tom in his best managerial tones.

"Yes, that's correct, right-turns."

"I don't follow," ventured Sam. "Where are these right-turns?"

"Exactly my point, dear boy. There aren't any."

At this point, a bewildered silence replaced the quick-fire quips – a sure sign that further interrogation was required.

"Where are there no right-turns, Nigel?" asked Tom with a wicked glint in his eye.

"Well, where do you think? Leicester of course! My God, you lot can be so slow."

"For the sake of accuracy, may I ask when, precisely, were you last in Leicester making these observations, Nigel?" enquired the landlord, who knew Nigel more by reputation than by acquaintance and was keen to find out more about this strange, shadowy figure who seemed to mix great intelligence with great insanity, in equal measures.

"Er, well let me see, must have been about thirty, no maybe thirty-five years ago. I was travelling (can't just think where I had been now) and I got a little bamboozled on the way home. I was following the signs and I saw a sign to Northampton. Now, knowing that Southampton is definitely in the south, I surmised that Northampton must be in the north so set off towards it." Sniggers started to breakout in darkened corners of the bar.

"Well, yes," snapped Nigel, "I now realise that it is all relative to where you start from but, by the time I realised my mistake, I was committed to my route and by some foul means found myself in Leicester. My excellent, nay infallible, in-built radar" (more sniggers from the subversive element) "told me I needed to turn right to get myself back on the right track." "Take more than a right turn in some uncharted Midland town to get him back on the right track," muttered Tom, but Nigel continued, undeterred.

"I was trapped in that god-forsaken town for hours on end, or so it seemed, and was beginning to think I would never escape."

"Well then, how did you?" broke in Sam, before anyone could start making snide comments about how Leicester should have tried harder. He rather liked Nigel.

"Initiative, dear boy, plain, good, old-fashioned initiative! It was late, no one much around, so I dodged down a few one-way streets (the wrong way, if you choose to believe the signs) and hey presto, I found the M1 and thence home."

A round of applause rippled around the merry drinkers.

"And that's the problem," he continued, unabashed. "Poor, old Dave has no initiative" ("Or driving convictions," added Tom, as a slightly too loud aside). "Hem, hem," glowered

Nigel, in Tom's direction, "and so he would be driving round and round until he was dizzy and desperate," ("Situation normal," Tom interjected again) "whereupon he would be easy pickings for any loose woman with no taste, no sense and no ambition. And of course, just like poor old Hansel and Gretel lost in the forest, once you have been seduced into the centre of Leicester, there is simply no way out."

"I didn't know he had picked up any hitchhikers," said Joe.

"What?" sang the crowd in an incredulous chorus. How had hitchhikers managed to sneak into the tale?

"Well this Handsmell and Greeta. How do you know about them, Nigel? I mean, I know you are the cleverest man in the room, but I can't see how you can possibly know that he picked them up, unless he's rung you, but I can't understand why he would…"

"Joe, shut up!" thankfully Tom, as his position demanded, had taken command of a rapidly deteriorating conversation. "It's a fairy story!"

"Oh my God, so he's picking up fairies now! Nigel, did he say if they had wings – or were they the other sort? You know, men, who, well you know, who…" Joe was getting himself all agitated and it was not a pretty sight.

Nigel stepped in. "Come on Joe, too much beer and excitement on an empty head is a bad combination. Come along, I'll take you home. You need your rest, which is why I came in here to find you in the first place."

Ahh, the mystery was about to unfold.

"Come on Nigel, do tell, before you leave."

"Well, it's very simple, rather like you lot!" Nigel was definitely grumpy.

"Well, I have just bought a brand new tractor, and it has cost me a great deal of money – it frightens me just to think of it. In fact it will have to work at least twenty-four hours a day to pay for itself. So I want my man Joe in tip-top condition when it arrives."

Nigel had a large farm on the outskirts of York and Joe was his right-hand man. What Joe lacked in brain-power, he more than made up for in sheer strength and willingness to please. That, allied to his massive inferiority complex, made him the perfect worker for Nigel. For Nigel, who had more intelligence than you could shake a stick at, (should you happen to be inclined to such shows of emotion) sadly had absolutely no common sense at all. All in all, they made the perfect combination.

Nigel turned on his heel and left, with Joe promising to follow very soon. Nigel's look of disgust indicated that he did not fully believe that this was going to happen in exactly the aforementioned timescale.

When the laughter subsided, attention turned back to 'Dave the Delivery' and his dilemma.

"Does anyone know owt about this lass?" asked the landlord. Silence was the loud reply.

"But why," continued Sam, still reeling from the former revelations, "would Dave leave home? I mean, I know he and his lass don't always see eye to eye, but I just assumed they were used to it and would shout and bawl for a while, and then make up."

"Well, it beats me," said Tom, shaking his head and rubbing his chin. I mean, we all know that 'Dave the Delivery' had a girl in every truck stop (Sam was slightly embarrassed that he seemed to be the only one who *didn't* know) and I think it's safe to say that, at some time or other, we have all secretly admired his stamina, and even at times envied his nerve, but I have to confess this has even taken me by surprise and, at my time of life, I'm not given to being surprised."

The landlord seemed to be getting a little impatient and it was then that Sam noticed he was anxiously thumbing through a tatty old exercise book, looking for a clean page.

"So," sighed mein host, as he slapped the book down on the

bar, "let's get it started." Everyone dutifully dipped into their pockets and produced a five pound note. Sam had no idea why, but he did the same and laid it on the bar with the others.

"You can go first, lad," Tom smiled at Sam; the landlord had his ballpoint poised, all eyes fixed eagerly on Sam, but Sam just stared, open-mouthed, at the scene.

"Well, lad, how long?"

"How long's what?" asked Sam and instantly regretted asking the question, as the most horrendous image formed in his mind, only to be backed up by the raucous "ooh er missus's" that reverberated around the taproom.

"Come on now, give the lad a chance. All you have to do is guess how long before he's back and acting as if nothing had ever happened," said Tom helpfully.

"What makes you think he will come back?" asked a dubious Sam.

"Because he always does! Admittedly he's never gone as far as Leicester before, but he'll be back, no doubt about it, and the one who guesses the nearest to how long he's been away, wins all those lovely fivers on that bar."

Sam looked a little perplexed. "Do you think we should take this so lightly? You know two, or maybe three, lives might be ruined here."

"A good drinking night might be ruined here, if you don't get a move on," grumbled some old man lurking menacingly at the end of the bar.

Sam, who had no experience of such goings on, had absolutely no idea how long it might take before a deserting delivery man became a prodigal pratt and returned home to resume domestic bliss (or was it blitz?).

"I don't know," he said, "I'll guess six months."

Again laughter raised the rafters.

"Now get real lad," chortled Tom. "We're talking lust here, not a custodial sentence at Her Majesty's pleasure."

"Well I bloody hope it's at somebody's pleasure," said Joe, "cos when he does come back he'll pay bloody dear for it! His lass is proper mad this time."

"She was proper mad to get involved with your Dave in the first place, if you ask me," laughed Tom, "but each to his own."

"Or somebody else's," said the landlord, "so can we please get on and get this book running; at this rate the daft bugger'll be back before we've all entered our guesses."

Now going sneaking off, so publicly, into a right-phobic Midland town, struck Sam as stretching the definition of daft a little further than he thought was good for it, but since moving up north, Sam was learning so much more about daft than he had imagined possible. However, he decided that he should indulge in a few more pints to help to clear his head. An interesting theory and one Sam thought worthy of further 'scientific' investigation.

During repeated experimentation with this theory, Sam had come to believe that indeed there was no problem so great that it could not be solved by several pints and a chat with the bar room sages. But for the sake of scientific correctness, it has to be noted here that in many cases, it was often found that the solution could lay open far more perplexing problems than the initial conundrum. But research had also shown that further and better dosages of the amber nectar could be relied on to sooth the most troubled of brows.

Indeed, as far as the revellers that night were concerned, the situation of Dave and his philandering was completely solved long before last orders were called, by the adoption of the simple mathematical equation: the sum of the beers down the neck, when multiplied by the improbability quotient, equals the sum of the headache and memory loss the next day.

And so it was that Sam, Tom and Joe left the pub that night in a haze of alcohol, laughter and utter bemusement; the landlord was left with a wad of used fivers and Dave simply remained lost, in lust, in Leicester.

The Tale of
Fred and Ginger

Ryan de Koning

"That fressher was and jolyer of array,

As to my doom, than is the month of may.

He syngeth, daunceth, passynge any man

That is, or was, sith that the world bigan."

The Franklin's Tale

Albert Stanley was walking towards the river. It was crisp. It was overcoat weather, at least in the shade, but as there was no wind, it was quite a delight in the sun. The sky was blue; there was a slight haze above the buildings. Two clouds caught Albert's eye, motionless, hovering in perfect symmetry. Albert paused for a moment and kept his face to the sky, closing his eyes and allowing the sun to shine down on him. He loved the way it caressed his skin, the warmth it gave on such a clear, cold day. Albert was on his way to meet his friend Ange, to celebrate the Spring Equinox. This was a special day to Albert, neither winter nor spring; it was an in-between day, twelve hours of daylight, twelve hours of darkness. Like two poling magnets, equal in strength, repelling, creating a void. It was a secret world, Albert's Neverland, and in it Albert was fearless. He liked to celebrate the Equinox by watching the flow of the River Ouse. He loved the river, he wanted to be like it; always moving, forever changing, journeying to never stop.

Albert walked down a path leading to St. Peter's Fields, at the back of Bootham. He had a spring in his step and he jigged whilst he walked. He stopped to look at fresh buds on the bushes, protected by sharp thorns. A blackbird gathered twigs for a new home amongst discarded beer cans. The path came to an end and opened up into playing fields, where people came with their families and pets. This was a part of York that wasn't often touched by the tourist. A rusty goal post stood at one end of the field. A dried, filled-in pond left to go wild, with unfamiliar roots sprouting strange, jagged grasses. The Minster loomed in the distance, an all-seeing eye over the City of York. In Albert's excitement he couldn't stop his mind from racing from thought to thought, like flicking through a book. Changing, aimless images raced by as if he were on a train. Albert was in total abandonment, following his own body, fluttering along like a butterfly, formless. He clenched his fists, tensed his leg muscles and stood on tiptoe. He craned his neck, thrusting his chin skywards. He was struck by a torrent of pleasure. Everything was perfect, every detail in perfect equilibrium. Albert began to skip. He didn't realise what he was doing at first, his legs just took him along and he allowed himself to be led. He was in the possession of this sweet spring morning. Zigzagging across the open space he felt like Fred Astaire; delicate and light-footed. He swooped and dipped, in and out with flowing movement. He floated like a bird; free, everything and nothing, twisting and turning. The corners of his mouth rose, stretched out, and a smile burst across his face.

Albert came to a halt. In the middle of the field a small girl was running around in circles, then marching and twisting. She was his Ginger Rogers. He watched her for a moment, watched as she bobbed her head like a chicken pecking grain, her lips all screwed up, a frown pulled over her eyes. She picked up a stick and waved it around, playing with her own shadow. Her eyes were ablaze, attracted to everything around her, absorbed in her senses, full of youth and growth. He skipped towards her. She giggled as he showed her his tap-dance and bowed.

"Good morning Madam," he said, pretending to tilt his hat, "Isn't it simply a delightful day?" He scanned the horizon, shielding his eyes from the sun with his hand.

"You're funny," she said.

"Would you care to dance?" he said, holding out his hand. She giggled once more before putting out her hand. He picked her up under the armpits and twirled her in the air. She smelt of freshly cut grass. She laughed aloud, spinning round and round. He touched his nose against hers, before placing her back on the ground. Albert was in purest joy. If there were a hill in York, he would surely climb it. He had surrendered himself, submerged his whole being into the openness of the day. He embraced all its flavours. Like Ginger Rogers beside him, he was in bliss for this one, single, glorious moment. He sucked in the air, hands on his hips like Peter Pan, he looked out over his empire.

In the distance he saw an approaching figure, a woman. She was coming towards them, picking up speed, like a juggernaut. Perhaps she was lost, looking for directions. She didn't seem too happy. Albert fixed a smile on his face. Meeting her eyes, Albert's smile increased – a natural trait, to smile at anyone looking directly at him. She didn't return his smile. He started to say "Hello," but only got as far as "H…" before she grabbed him by the throat, baring her teeth and began to shake him. Albert gasped for breath and pulled at her fingers, as if he was undoing his tie. His head was being jerked backwards and flung forwards. Sharp pains went up the back of his neck and into his skull. Albert did his best to stay on his feet. Next, the woman took hold of his hair and began yanking with gusto. He had seen it coming but was too shocked to defend himself. Everything was happening so fast. He thought about raising his hands to protect his face, but as he considered this she took to his throat again, digging in her nails and ripping flesh. She knew where all the holes were in his defence and kept jabbing at them. Albert's mind was buzzing with unfinished sentences, "What if I…" She slapped him. "Maybe I should…" She elbowed him in the throat. "I could always…" She shook him back and forth, gripping his ears. "That's not really…" She rapped her knuckles down on his nose, "Jesus Christ that…" She pushed her thumb in his eye. "For the love of…!" She dug her nails into his collarbone. Albert was drowning, hit by wave after continuous wave. He tried to understand the words behind the woman's constant screaming. She ripped open his shirt, then pounded on the top of his head with her fist. He felt himself dropping to his knees, the weight of her hands pushing him downwards. He raised his hand to cover his face, as she kicked him in the stomach. This didn't seem fair, thought Albert. She had a clear head start and he wasn't even prepared. Trying to stay afloat, his arms flapping, gasping for air, his body came to a halt as the grass moved closer to slap him in the face.

Albert was lying down on his chest with his head to the side. There was stillness. He remained there for a few moments waiting for the final blow to end it, but it never came. His neck was feeling stiff and he needed to move. Behind him he could hear a voice asking if someone was all right. He licked his lips, that were crusted with blood from his nose, and whispered that he was fine now. He began to move his hands and arms, making sure they worked, and slowly raised his neck and shoulders. He eased up on his arms, turned onto his back and sat up on his elbows. Squinting, he saw the woman crouching, her arms wrapped around the child. Another woman stood to one side.

"How is she? She okay?"

"One more second with that beast, I don't know what..." she tailed off, shaking her head, gripping the girl tightly. Albert frowned and stared at the two women. He looked down at his torn shirt, scratches across his narrow chest, and then covered himself with his blazer. His nose was tender, his bottom lip slightly swollen. Blood was still oozing out of his nose and drying around his mouth. He sniffed and tasted blood at the back of his throat. He reached into his pocket and brought out a tissue, and dabbed it at the entrance of his right nostril. His head was throbbing and his shirt collar kept catching against his ripped neck. He touched his neck lightly with his fingers. It felt as though it had been ploughed; it was torn up and raw.

Suddenly a shadow covered him. He saw the silhouette of a man. By squinting Albert could just about make out the eyes. He seemed hungry. "You're dead mate," the man said. Albert wondered if he was dead now or would be dead later: probably soon, with the aid of this fine gentleman. The man prodded him in the chest with his finger, almost pushing

Albert over. Dead later he thought. He sat up, readjusted his blazer. He pulled back his shoulders and pushed out his chest. He tried to ignore the titan eyeballing him. He picked at the grass, rubbing it between his fingers. Albert considered his position; in front of him he had a lady consoling the crazy woman, who had her arms wrapped around Ginger Rogers. To his right he had a giant of a man who wanted, so it seemed, to fight also. Wasn't it winner stay on? Surely the mad woman won? Surely she was back in the ring?

A mobile phone started ringing; it was the giant's. The man answered and turned away from Albert to begin a conversation about household insulation. Albert watched him for a while, then looked back at Ginger and the two women. Behind him was an open field. He raised his knees and rocked himself forwards to a crouching position. He looked at the man and then at the ladies once more with their backs to him. A chance. He turned on the ball of his foot and pushed off into a run. His legs felt like they were moving in different directions, arms flapping, head back, mouth wide open in a silent scream. His muscles were clenching, contracting, contorting. Like a screwed up piece of paper, he was slowly unwrapping. He ran and he ran, his eyes watering, the cold air brushing against his face.

He reached the river and followed the path towards Lendal Bridge. The path, still covered in silt from recent flooding, made Albert almost slip and fall. Unconscious of his surroundings, Albert followed the path until he reached the Museum Gardens, where Ange was sitting on a bench looking at the water. "You're late," she said, without turning to face him. He collapsed onto the bench next to her, panting. Albert swallowed deeply, a stitch rooted deep in his ribs. "I got distracted." Leaning forwards, bent over, breathing deeply, he wiped his lips, his mouth full of thick saliva. There was nobody following, the path was clear; he felt safe, he was with

Ange. She was still facing the river. She was wearing a green woollen hat and a wax jacket. The left-hand pocket was sagging with the weight of the thick paperback lodged in it. She resembled a pile of clothes waiting to go in the washing machine. Albert slid back against the bench and gazed at the river. The light caught every ripple and sparkled before Albert's eyes. He watched as the sun danced for him.

The riverside was virtually devoid of activity. The breeze could only just be detected as it rattled through the trees. A couple walked by and stopped, as the woman re-arranged her husband's collar. A few pigeons gathered, looking forward to breakfast from the local bread-givers. Albert sank further into the seat, his face puffy, his head throbbing, the pulse beating steadily in his temples. His right eye was bloodshot and weeping. On the bridge of his nose a bruise had developed like a dirty mark. Dried blood formed one half of a handlebar moustache. Ange stretched her arms half-heartedly and looked at Albert. Resting her hands on her knees, she half-closed her eyes to examine him.

"You don't seem your usual self today, Albert," she said, crossing her legs. "You done something to your hair?" Albert touched his hair, it was sticking up like horns, sore at the root.

"I'd rather not talk about it," he sniffed, putting his hand to his mouth and lightly nibbling on his knuckle with his lips. What had he done? Why had that woman attacked him? He looked at Ange, she at him. He smelt the skin on the back of his hand; it smelt of the sun, sweet as bacon. He circled the top of his hand with his lips, only just touching, and he breathed-in the cooked air. He closed his eyes and allowed his fingers to stroke every bobble of raised skin on his face. Around the nose, pressing ever so slightly against his eyelids; his warm breath rising in the air, touching his palms. He had been devoured.

"You don't seem to be in the mood for Equinox river watching. Perhaps a cup of tea?" Ange said. He looked at her and in a whisper said, "Spring is anarchy."

They walked along the river, away from the gardens with its ruined Abbey as defeated as Albert. At Museum Street they entered a café. It was busy. Albert kept his head down, not wishing to make eye contact with anyone. A lady drinking a cup of Earl Grey stopped in mid-conversation and motioned her friend to look at Albert.

"I don't think coming in here was such a good idea," Albert said.

"Nonsense," replied Ange, sitting down. "It's just what you need, a nice hot cup of tea." They sat at the back corner of the room, near the entrance to the kitchen, and watched as the waitresses came back and forth, the doors swinging. Albert caught the eye of a chef in the kitchen through the gap in the doors. A snapshot, then he was gone. To one side of the door there was a table with condiments arranged on it, and a radio playing a tune by Glenn Miller. A waitress took their order and returned a moment later, sliding a tray onto the table with a pot of tea and two teacakes. Pouring their tea, Ange began staring at Albert, tilting her head sideways to see him from different angles.

"I can't put my finger on it," she said, "but, there's something not quite right." Albert ignored her. It wasn't just Ange looking. The stares had become contagious and were spreading from table to table. Whispers gathered pace around the room, like a fog that engulfed him; their vulture-like appetites were consuming him. Albert wanted to run away. But he couldn't move. Too many eyes. Ange didn't notice anything, she only drew more attention with her constant fidgeting and rummaging amongst sachets of sauces on the table. He stared into his tea, stirring in heaped teaspoons of sugar until it was almost thick, like syrup. His spoon scraped the bottom of the cup, as his tea turned into a whirlpool of darkness; round and round it went like a curving snake.

"Why were you running back there?" Ange said, adjusting her woollen hat so that it covered her eyebrows.

"I was late."

"You never run," she said, "I've never seen you run and you're always late."

Albert shrugged his shoulders, he wanted to forget; his own questions haunted him enough. What did he do to deserve that attack? He shook his head whilst Ange thought of more questions.

"You looked," she said, "like you were running away from something, rather than running towards me."

"You weren't even looking at me, you were looking at the river." Raising her index finger and wagging it slightly she replied,

"I see more than you think."

Albert wanted to be somewhere else, another world, another time – away from people attacking him, badgering him. He sat up and pulled in his chair. Pushing his teacake away from him, he rested on his elbows, his attention disappearing once more into the depths of his teacup.

"I wonder what the weather will be like tomorrow," Ange said, touching his arm with her hand. "I'll check the radio." Albert didn't look up from his drink. He liked the way the steam made his face wet. He picked at the rim of his cup, using his thumbnail to remove old tea stains. In the meantime Ange had got up, grabbed the radio and put it in the middle of their table. Changing channels, the music was lost to the news.

"York City police are asking for any information regarding an attack on a seven year old girl in the playing fields behind St. Peter's School this morning. The attacker was witnessed wooing his victim with a skipping display…" Albert reached over and turned the radio off. He picked it up and put it on his lap. He held on to it, gripping as tightly as he could.

"That's what it was," Albert said to himself, looking blankly at the table. "You know, you can't touch a child these days without someone…" He broke off and looked at Ange, her face all confused. "I was dancing, just dancing. Why do I feel guilty? Why should I?"

"What have you done?" The room was silent. Albert noticed everybody in the café had stopped and they were all waiting for his next move. He scratched the side of his head absently. A man on the next table reached into his pocket, pulled out a mobile phone and began to dial. With his head in his hands Albert said,

"What does it matter, they've already made up their minds."

The Farmer's Tale

Andrew Jenkinson

"As whan a man hath been in povre estaat,

And clymbeth up and wexeth fortunat,

And there abideth in prosperitee

Swich thyng is gladsom, as it thynketh m,

And of swich thyng were goodly for to telle."

The Nun's Priest's Prologue

On the edge of bustling York there is a small rural idyll; a tiny piece of countryside that time has mostly forgotten. Here, production of food is a way of life and the noise of the city seems a lifetime away. On the village farm, almost a hundred beautiful black-and-white Friesian cows graze serenely on lush speckled meadows of clover and thistles, and the occasional scarlet poppy.

However, before everything changed, the lane leading to Sparrowfart Farm was full of monumental, bone-shaking potholes. In fact, it was rumoured that you could see these potholes from outer space. One could imagine the astronauts joking on each completion of the earth, "Look at those hideous potholes in the lane leading to Sparrowfart Farm!"

They were certainly no laughing matter to the village postman. Nevertheless, over the years he had worked out a sequence of manoeuvres to avoid the holes. These manoeuvres were firmly locked away in his head with as much precision as his old army numbers. It went like this. Swing the steering wheel left then immediately right, straight on for ten yards, right again and then sharp left to avoid the longest deepest hole. Straight on for twelve yards, hard right, count to four, then a long curving left. And so on for the entire length of the lane. He eventually arrived at the farmhouse in one piece, with just a niggling headache or churned-up stomach to show for his daily adventure.

Old Joe Underwood was invariably there each morning to receive the post, even if it was only a couple of farming mail-shots. "Time you got that lane fixed, Joe," grunted the postman, handing him several bulky items of mail.

"I'm only a poor farmer," pleaded Joe, in his thick Yorkshire accent, "how am I going to afford a new tarmac road?"

"My boss says we might have to stop delivering mail to Sparrowfart Farm," responded the postman sharply.

Joe's eyes twinkled, "Look Bill, you know you get a thrill zig-zagging down that lane in your little van!"

"Aye, maybe I do," replied the postie, "but those holes are getting bigger, and I'm not so nimble on the steering wheel as I used to be." Joe had repeatedly heard the same old story from the post office in the village. "More of the same junk mail tomorrow?" he boomed, as he turned to go back towards the farmhouse. Defeated, Bill returned to his van.

"I reckon it will take a summons to get those holes filled in," he shouted. "Some hopes," mumbled Joe as the post van sped off to do battle with the obstacles again. He flipped through the post and, seeing nothing of importance, almost skipped into the farmhouse kitchen.

His sons, Eddie and Philip, were still hard at work in the splendid new herringbone milking parlour. It had been installed less than a year and was fully automated, leaving the boys little to do. They always joked that now the cows could almost milk themselves. Every morning the cows waited in the collecting yard for their turn to enter. They invariably went in in the same sequence, except for some freshly calved heifer that decided to push in early. This was always thwarted by one of the older cows nosing her sternly out of the way.

The boys were coming towards the end of the morning milking and were feeling exhausted.

"Just what are we doing here, Eddie?" asked Philip, washing down a rather pendulous, dirty udder, "up at the crack of dawn, it's not natural."

"It weren't so bad when times were good," moaned Eddie, as he released another cow into the yard. "Now the job's not worth getting out of bed for. I'd be better off at the chocolate factory."

"Yeah, the supermarkets are milking us," quipped Philip, "we were getting more for our milk five years ago."

"Just running to stand still," continued Eddie, shouting above the steady, rhythmic noise of the vacuum pump that drew the milk from the cows' udders. Suddenly one of the large cows above Eddie lifted its tail ramrod straight and squirted a stream of excrement in a perfect arc, splattering on the concrete floor. Like the professional he was, Eddie ducked quickly, treating it as an occupational hazard. The offending material was quickly swept away into one of the water channels, leaving the parlour as pristine and as hygienic as ever.

The white, bubbly, creamy milk soon filled the large overhead glass containers by each cow stall, squirting in the liquid to the pulses of the vacuum. A big black-and-white animal ambled its way into the parlour without a care in the world and made for the vacant space, a cascade of dairy nuts shot into the trough. "That the last?" inquired Philip, sounding tired.

"That's the one," responded Eddie with glee, knowing that breakfast wasn't far away. "I'm starving, I could eat a steak!" Just then another of the outgoing cows let out a deep-throated bellow, "Not you, old girl," laughed Eddie.

Back in the farmhouse, Joe Underwood had perused the post at the large kitchen table and was violently slurping his second mug of coffee. Joe's wife, Gladys, was still busy at the Aga putting the final touches to a massive breakfast fry-up. The table, despite being extremely untidy, was laid out at one end for the boys when they came in. A selection of multi-coloured cartons stood amid a large spillage of cornflakes. Slowly Joe leafed through a weekly farming magazine and made a few grunts and groans about the article headlines.

"You sound constipated," said Gladys, resigned to this performance each morning.

"Just skimming through this article about diversification," grumbled Joe, "be simple enough if we could grow a crop of diversification in a field somewhere." He reluctantly read on, "Says we farmers must find another source of income to make ends meet."

"Look at Jack down at Fulford," brightened his wife, "you know how they've those holiday homes and are making a good living, apparently."

"Humbug," shouted Joe, "we're farmers, we're meant to till the soil, produce the food to fill bellies."

"And now we're supposed to be paid for looking after the countryside," smiled Gladys, putting a large platter of fried breakfast into the Aga.

"Us farmers have always been the custodians of the countryside," raged Joe, "if it wasn't for us, the countryside wouldn't be worth these townies rushing out to litter it up each weekend." Gladys poured herself a cup of tea and sat round the table, taking the weight off her feet. She usually made do with a couple of rounds of toast and marmalade, before trying to keep the large farmhouse looking tidy. Joe finished reading his farming magazine and skidded it across the table, where it gently nudged a bowl of sugar. The sugar spoon jumped up and spread a small arc of crystals across the table top. He grunted and searched his jacket pockets for his tobacco tin, before taking out a fancy briar pipe from his top pocket.

"You're not lighting that filthy thing," scolded his wife, "not at the breakfast table."

"Only pleasure I gets in life now. I can see our dairy cows going the way of the dodo," he slumped back in his chair and sucked on an unlit pipe.

Meanwhile the 7.l5am train from York was ten minutes late and packed with passengers heading towards London. It was just picking up speed after its stop in York station and passing through Copmanthorpe. The refreshment trolley had started its journey rattling down the centre aisle and a few people were purchasing sandwiches and soft drinks. Businessmen and women had open laptops on the tables and were typing unseen details into the voracious machines. Ubiquitous mobile phones rang themselves crazy from all quarters. Business-like conversations, insane conversations, and even raunchy conversations, went on amidst the other silent passengers.

Richard Oldfield sat intently watching through the window of his carriage. He had done this each morning for the last few days, while the germ of an idea gradually took shape. Just after York station he became highly animated; it was his signal to look through the window and watch the countryside flash by. Yes, there they were again, those huge black-and-white beasts looking magnificent. Sometimes they were just wandering into the field from the farmyard after milking. Other times they were already grazing in the field, glad to be away from all the machinery of the milking parlour. This spot was absolutely perfect, thought Richard, alongside a main railway track and with a major road running along another side. He stifled an urge to shout out in triumph, but couldn't help a broad grin spreading across his face. Yes, you've really hit the jackpot this time, you've really cracked it! He punched his fist into his other, open hand. His fellow passengers wondered for his sanity.

For almost twenty years he had built up a prosperous and well-respected advertising agency in York. It had many high profile, blue-chip companies on its books and, from a small office in Pocklington, it had grown into a large organisation without feeling the need to move down to London. Richard was aware that he hadn't had an original idea since the one about mushy peas a few years previously. He smiled, thinking how mushy peas had put the Oldfield Advertising Agency on the map. Now he was going to make his fortune from cows. He had spent the week commuting to see a valued client in Doncaster in order to tie up a few details for a television campaign. But once this package had been signed and sealed, he could channel all his energy into this project. He removed a small notepad from his briefcase, made a few notes and then rang his secretary in the York office to undertake a spot of detective work.

The following week, Richard Oldfield sat in his opulent office within the shadow of the vast, majestic bulk of York Minster. He was surrounded by tasteful glass-fronted posters taken from his most successful advertising campaigns. The huge leather-topped desk dominated the room like some angular beached whale. Two computer screens flickered away within arm's reach behind him, while a huge plasma television screen covered the entire wall. E-mails, faxes and other sheets of paper and manuscripts lay in neat rows on the desktop. The in and out trays bulged with urgent business. He slowly placed his elbows on the desk, put his palms together and steepled his fingers. Deep in thought, he was interrupted by his secretary, who came in and delicately sat on a chair opposite the desk.

"Ah Suzy, I called you in to thank you personally for your sterling efforts over the last few days."

"All part of the job, Richard. It really wasn't difficult," she smiled, crossing her long legs.

"I still can't imagine how you managed to track them down so quickly, and come up with all that information."

"Used my initiative. Voters register, council records and a bit of digging from a farmer friend who lives in Askham Bryan."

"Well, no matter how you managed to come up with all that, well done. I'll see you get a little bonus out of this, we all will."

"By the way, I saw to the letter myself, it went off by registered post. I assume they would have received it today. We will have to see if they take the bait."

"Oh Suzy, you're an angel."

Back on Sparrowfart Farm, the Underwoods' farmhouse looked rather sad at the end of the lane. It was probably only the woodworm holding hands that stopped it from tumbling down. The thatch sagged like a poor soufflé. Inside the kitchen there was a palpable buzz of excitement. The entire Underwood family were called together for a mini conference over the contents of a very strange letter. Joe sat at the head of the table and again put the facts to the family. "Not much to go on, is it?" he squinted hard at the letter. "The Oldfield Advertising Agency wants to know if we can we go to their office in York, where we will hear 'something to our advantage'. "

"I could understand it from a solicitor," said Gladys thoughtfully, "but what's an advertising agency want with us farmers?"

"Sounds intriguing," chirped in Eddie, "'something to our advantage'. I like it."

"What have we got that could possibly be of interest to them?" questioned Philip, still rather doubtful.

"Wants us to visit their office next week; if not convenient can we contact them to make alternative arrangements," mumbled Joe, still deep in thought and confusion. The only one to make instant decisions (which usually turn out to be perfectly sound) was Gladys. With no hesitation she shouted, "We go!"

"We go!" they all chorused.

Just as Great Peter in York Minster boomed out eleven o'clock the following week, they entered the splendid portals of the Oldfield Advertising Agency. With some trepidation, the Underwoods announced themselves at the plush reception desk and were told to wait in the comfortable atrium. Hardly had they sat down when Suzy arrived, smiling beautifully and offering to escort them up to Richard Oldfield's office. Climbing a flight of ornate, winding stairs and moving past several large, open plan offices did nothing to calm their anxieties. Richard Oldfield was sitting nervously in his large leather chair when Suzy knocked and ushered in the Underwoods. He quickly stood and shook hands with the family and waved them to sit in the comfortable chairs set out especially for them.

"I'm so pleased you could attend," he smiled, "please feel free to make yourselves at home." There was a continuing silence, not helped by Gladys jiggling in her chair, trying to relax.

"Yes, well, I expect you're all wondering why I've called you here today!" Still silence. The Underwoods were rather uncertain how to open the conversation.

"As you must know by now, we are a large advertising agency representing several large companies and responsible for many slogans and advertising campaigns."

"Just where do we come in?" boomed Joe, suspicious. Richard cleared his throat.

"I've had this wizard idea."

"Wizard? Such as in Harry Potter?" grinned Eddie. The head of the agency laughed and continued, "No. No. It's those cows of yours, I'd sort of like to borrow them."

"You can't borrow our cows!" cried Gladys, horrified. "Who ever heard of such a thing!"

"How do you mean 'borrow'?" asked Philip, trying to restore dignity, "We ain't no rental company."

"What if I told you," said Richard, almost confidentially, "that this agency would build an advertising campaign around them. It would be of huge financial benefit to you – we'd pay handsomely."

"Just how handsome?" inquired Joe, gruffly.

"Now that's all open to negotiation when you know the full

implications." The family was stunned by these revelations and took a while to digest it all. Joe looked at his wife, then at his sons and then expelled a great deal of air. He opened his mouth as if to say something, but nothing came out.

"Hadn't you better tell us the full story?" asked Philip, "and perhaps we can reach a decision."

"Especially if we're talking money," smirked Eddie, "cos' there's not much in farming these days."

The negotiations went on for hours. The Underwoods drove a hard bargain, since they felt they had the upper hand. At the conclusion of the frenetic meeting, they were excited by the venture and realised it would put Sparrowfart Farm, and the city of York, on the map. The meeting over, they all shook hands and the Underwoods could already imagine the smile on their bank manager's face.

"Thank you all," beamed an ecstatic Richard Oldfield, bursting with bonhomie. "Lovely doing business with you, I'll have my legal department draw up a proper contract and we can take it from there."

Three weeks later the momentous day arrived. All the hard work had been sorted out, the numerous advertising contracts with a multitude of companies signed and sealed. The Oldfield Advertising Agency was on a roll, and the Underwoods were permanently smiling, having watched their overdraft wiped out in one go. The day dawned sunny and warm, and after an early morning milking, the cows looked in tremendous shape. For several days the entire advertising agency had been encamped on the farm with the VIPs from the various companies that had signed up to the new venture. The Underwoods were in their Sunday best, looking spotless and presentable for a change. Prompted by the agency, many television companies had descended on the farm to beam two-minute spots into their news programmes. Almost fifty people were working back in the cattle sheds, making sure everything was looking absolutely perfect. The cows were subjected to intensive beauty treatments by some of the top beauticians, who groomed the cattle like A-list film stars.

Suddenly a claxon sounded to start the proceedings. Reluctantly, and very slowly, the cows ambled their way into the field. Each cow had a large advertising jacket slung over their body, and every jacket extolled the attributes and the virtues of buying a particular product. There were large, colourful adverts for chocolates; for various toiletries; a whole range of shops and supermarkets; a multitude of instant foods; nourishing foods; and for junk foods. Cows had adverts on both sides of the jacket, showing brands of dog food, washing powders, various makes of cars and even the merits of the softest toilet roll. Some had pictures of furniture and bedding, a complete range of carpets and electrical goods. There were even adverts for the local area, extolling the exciting delights of a visit to York; trains at the National Railway Museum or Viking history at the Jorvik Museum; the Castle Museum or a trip down Kirkgate; the Yorkshire Museum or a boat ride down the River Ouse.

An audible gasp of incredulity went up from the assembled guests to see this fanciful sight. Passing trains whistled loudly and passengers crowded to the windows to watch the uniqueness of this historic event in advertising. Cars slowed down, or even stopped on the main road for drivers to take a longer look. Many rubbed their eyes, not quite believing what they saw. A tailback of traffic soon developed on the road, and several minor shunts occurred before the police from Fulford police station arrived to restore order. Evening Press reporters thronged the site, snapping up the splendour of the phenomenon and interviewing anyone who was even remotely connected to the event. So if you are travelling by train, or by car, just outside the City of York, keep your eyes peeled – you might just see some walking Moo-bile ads...

A Tale of
Two Sisters

Rachael Forsyth

"After Pride wol I speken of the foule synne

Of Envye, which that is, as by the word

of the philosophre,

'sorwe of oother mannes prosperitee..."

The Parson's Tale

I hate my younger sister. From her perfect size eight figure to the way her hair invariably seems glamorous; Paige appears untarnished by life. She gets all the attention and, no matter what I do, she shuns me from the spotlight. But not anymore. Now it's my turn to take centre stage. For once in my life I'm better than my younger sister.

My older sister and I have never got on. No matter what I did, it would never be good enough. For some reason Tiffany can't see past my good looks to the person inside. She is beautiful, but pushes others away with her foolish pride. I hate her for pushing me away and yet I love her. She is my sister after all.

The sunshine hit the droplet of water, refracting it into small rainbows that glistened in the early morning light. Each bead of water shone like a diamond on a jeweller's cloth. With a swipe their allure was abolished; natural beauty ended with a quick brush of fabric. Tiffany trailed the cloth along the silver metallic surface, oblivious to the miracles of nature that clung to her car. Wiping the bonnet, she sighed and lovingly ran her hand over the paintwork. Smiling, she remembered the first time she had driven her Jaguar XK from the showroom. The power thrilled her and she had fallen in love with every curve of its body. It had taken her two years and too many cases to pay for it, but now it was hers. Her shining steed. Sighing louder, she unlocked the boot and crammed the last matching case into the too-small space. *It's going to be a long weekend*, she thought grimly.

Tiffany's mood lifted as soon as she got onto the motorway. With the air-conditioning and the radio up high, she was almost able to forget where she was going. But, as always, the journey was over too soon. She pulled into the drive and pressed the horn. With a single glance she was able to see every weed that plagued the garden and every chip in the paintwork that had been neglected. Tiffany honked the horn once more and tapped her finger angrily on the steering wheel. Fuming, she waited; her sister was late as usual.

Paige stepped out of the door in a flurry of books and bags. She tried to ignore her sister's icy stare and calmly collected the papers she'd dropped. Waving apologetically she walked over to the car. "Hey sis."

"You'll have to stick those on the back seat, Paige. There's no more room in the boot."

"Travelling light again, Tiff?" Paige giggled. "Let's get this show on the road."

"This show's been ready for ten minutes," Tiffany snapped, pulling out of the drive.

"Well if you will insist on being early."

"I'm not early, the time is precisely…"

"Look, do we have to start our holiday the same way we do every year?" Paige sighed, slipping her fashionable sunglasses on.

"Well everything else about the holiday is the same, so why vary the conversation?"

"Fine. Well, no doubt you can remember my half of the conversation as well, so you amuse yourself. I'm gonna have fifty winks." Paige closed her eyes; a wry smile touching her lips. She had got the last word in, knowing how much it infuriated her sister.

The motorway slowed to the usual Bank Holiday crawl and Tiffany cursed for not taking the last slip road. Paige was scribbling furiously on an open exercise book that she balanced precariously on her lap; the sound of the fountain pen grated on Tiffany's patience. "Do you have to do that now?"

"Yes."

"Well don't. It's annoying." The sun's rays beat mercilessly against the cars and even Tiffany's air conditioning wasn't able to dispel the sticky warmth that clung to their skin and shortened their already strained tempers. Paige sighed.

"Are you going to tell me what's bothering you, or are you going to carry on giving me the silent treatment and the odd verbal insult?" Tiffany kept quiet, her lower lip jutting out. "Really, Tiff, my year six class behaves better than you do sometimes."

"Look, I'm sorry. I'm just hot and bothered. It's too warm to be driving today, let's stop and get a drink."

The sun gracefully slipped behind a cloud, bringing blessed relief to the scorched lands below. Tiffany stormed back to the car, fuming that her sister could take so long drinking the same cup of coffee. "I think we'll take the next slip road; the motorway will be at a standstill now."

"Whatever Tiff, you're driving." Paige shrugged.

"That's right and, for future reference, I'll be the one driving for the remainder of this trip."

"You're not still sore about last time are you?"

"Do you know how much it cost me to get that scratch covered?"

"I offered to pay for it..."

"What? On your wages?" Tiffany scoffed.

"We can't all be top notch defence lawyers, can we?"

"If you hadn't settled for that teaching job instead of completing your law degree..."

"I didn't settle for anything. As difficult as it might be for you to understand, I do enjoy my job – which is more than you can say about yours."

"You actually enjoy teaching snotty-nosed little brats?"

"Yes, it's called job satisfaction." Tiffany scoffed again and each sister lapsed into silence once more; welcoming the uncomfortable situation like a well-worn blanket.

Time will always bring change; for better or for worse. As the time grew on, the sun began to tilt in the sky and the world around them changed. Hills rose and fell and the land grew more sparse and isolated. Paige smiled as the land around her transformed into one she knew and loved. Her heart skipped a beat, as the great cooling towers loomed over them as they passed by; they were almost there. Every year they made the same trip and every year she fell more in love with the Yorkshire countryside; from the trundling tractors to the modern architecture. Tiffany scowled as Paige wound the window down and inhaled deeply.

"The air's no different up here, you know." Paige turned to her sister, her cheeks aglow and her eyes bright.

"Oh it is. It is and you know it." Tiffany grumbled under her breath, but she knew that it was true. She didn't love the scenery or the animals, but she did like it. Not that she would admit it to Paige. The pace was so much slower that Tiffany found time to stop and reflect. It was the only time she allowed herself to sit and look back on the year that had passed. Despite their grievances, neither sister would admit to wanting to visit York by themselves. Their past was the same and, despite their disagreements both sisters chose to weave their future with the other. Two halves of the same coin will always disagree, but without one there could be no other.

Clouds drew in from the north, bringing with them the rain and bitter cold that all holidaymakers wished to be without. It wouldn't be a Bank Holiday without the downpours. Drearily they drove into the city centre, both overwhelmed with different feelings. Paige watched in awe as the Minster rose on the horizon, its great peaks reaching towards the sky. A building so large and grand demanded respect, and it was dutifully given. Tiffany tried to hold back a shudder as they drove through the great archways within the Bar Walls, the great stonework barring intruders' entry, as well as her escape. Her nerve was unsettled already by the graves that they had passed (the bodies within them consumed by the plague) which now stood as a tourist attraction.

Raindrops fell faster as they pulled down the narrow street and parked in the hotel car park. Each sister said a silent curse to the god of shopping, for letting her pack so many clothes. They struggled from the car and hurried up the cobbled streets to the hotel, both wishing that they had packed a coat. For a surprising change to their holiday routine, Tiffany had decided that they should stay in a hotel rather than at Aunty Margie's. She hated the décor for a start and sharing a room with Paige, without having a bar to escape to, was her idea of hell. They were soon settled in the room and, after a few moments of unpacking, Tiffany declared that she needed a drink and left to find the bar. Paige watched her leave and stepped over to the window, focussing on the pattern of raindrops that danced across the surface of the Ouse. Sighing, she turned back and began folding her own clothes before attacking the mess Tiffany had left, pointing out to herself that she was once again cleaning up after her sister.

A fire crackled softly, lighting the leather sofas that littered the room. Confidently Tiffany strode to the bar and started tapping her manicured nails irritably as she waited for the barman to appear. A door opened and Tiffany glared, about to chastise him for keeping her waiting, but the moment she saw him her mouth faltered. The barman seemed to float on air. He smiled as he glided towards her, his dark brown hair framed his face and his eyes sparkled beneath a light pair of glasses. Delicately the man took her order and tenderly poured her a drink. Peering over the rim of the wine glass, Tiffany gazed into his eyes; they seemed to flicker in the light. A voice called out, shattering the silence. "I'm off, Andrew. Don't work too hard." Andrew laughed and called back that he wouldn't. "Unless you're going to be demanding, that is?" he said softly. Tiffany giggled, something she hadn't done since she was a young girl. "Well, I have been known to be demanding. But I may make an exception for you."

"That's very kind of you." Andrew walked round the bar and sat on the stool next to her, bringing a bottle of wine and another glass with him. "I hope I'm not keeping you from anything."

"Not at all. I'm here all by myself."

A gust of wind caressed the paper and carried it high; making it dance amongst the flowers in the surrounding fields. Teasingly it lifted and dropped it again, tempting all around to try and snag its new-found prize. "Goddamn it Paige, I knew I shouldn't have let you drive!" Puffing, Paige climbed over the wire fence, wincing as her trouser caught on one of the barbs. Glancing over her shoulder, she saw that their map had settled further on in the field. Scowling, she knew it would be taken away as soon as she got close enough. *I won't play with you any longer*, she thought bitterly. "How are we going to get out of here without a map?" Tiffany wailed, folding her arms tightly across her chest. Paige stared at her sister levelly.

"If you want the map, feel free to go and get it. I'm not chasing a piece of paper halfway round the county." Tiffany stuck her bottom lip out and sulkily polished the bonnet with her sleeve.

"If I'd driven…"

"Well you didn't. I had to. There's that much alcohol in your system you're still unfit to drive." Paige had secretly rejoiced when Tiffany came stumbling into the room in the early hours of the morning and spent most of the night being sick. She knew Tiffany was scowling beneath her designer-labelled sunglasses, so pretended not to enjoy driving the car. As they weren't staying with Aunty Margie, Paige thought it only polite to visit. Except after ten years of spending a weekend with Aunty Margie in her country cottage, neither of them could remember the way to her house and needed a map to get there. Paige remembered the scenery that they should have passed; the quaint little villages with the picturesque streams that ran in front of the houses and the high, flat pastures littered with sheep. But she didn't recognize anything on the road they were travelling. Due to the speed at which Paige had driven, Tiffany's already dubious navigating skills had become confused. They had soon taken a wrong turn and found themselves driving down a winding track that had grass growing as high on the verges as it did down the centre of the road. Calling that she would be back once she had found help from a nearby farm, Paige quickly slipped down the lane. Wincing, she heard Tiffany shriek. A stream of obscenities ruptured the countryside. Paige increased her speed, as she knew that Tiffany had found the scratch she had once again put in the paintwork of her beloved car. She only hoped that she would be back before Tiffany noticed that the car was also out of petrol.

As soon as Paige could no longer hear Tiffany's wailing, she was able to relax. The day was pleasant, but the heat from the sun on her back made her uncomfortable. Flies buzzed angrily around her and, despite the constant bites they gave her, Paige smiled. In the distance she could make out the buildings of a small farm. She hobbled faster, the graze on her leg aching, knowing that the less time she took the less of a roasting she would get from Tiffany when she returned. A chorus of barking announced her arrival at the farm gate and two large dogs ran over, snarling at her behind the bars. A voice hollered for them to get down and a figure stepped out of the barn, raising an arm at her.

"Come in. Don't worry, they're quite safe." The man stepped back into the building, the dogs following in his wake. Paige followed him into the barn and was relieved by the cool temperature that seeped from the walls. "Nasty scratch you have there." Paige blushed and told him it was nothing, sitting on a bale of hay as she spoke.

"Glad to hear it." Resting in the cool interior of the building, Paige began to relax as she watched him spread hay across the floor, the young man's muscles flexing beneath his shirt. Even in the dimness of the barn, Paige could see the man's sky-blue eyes sparkle beneath the light-rimmed glasses he wore. Unable to suppress a sigh, Paige leant back and watched him finish his work. Gradually, as the conversation began to flow, all thoughts of her sister left her mind.

Tiffany realised what a roast chicken felt like when she woke from her nap. The heat of the day had baked the leather interior of her car, the seats sticking to her bare skin. Grimacing in the mirror, she saw her face had turned red and puffed up. It took her ages to straighten her static-filled hair; with each vicious swipe of her comb Tiffany cursed her sister. She cursed her for scratching her car for the second time and for getting them both lost in the middle of nowhere. Pounding the steering wheel, she screamed as she realised that they were also out of petrol. *Guess it's up to me to solve this problem,* she thought bitterly, *as always.* Her pace swift and her mind set, Tiffany started out in the same direction as Paige. Glancing at her watch, she stifled any concerns she had for her sister. *She'd better be injured or unconscious,* she thought, *because she will be when I find her.*

Sipping her coffee from a thermos lid, Paige looked up and giggled inwardly. *Look, I know he's gorgeous,* she told herself, *let's just take this one step at a time.* But her mind had a habit of getting ahead of itself. It read meanings into every similarity they had between them and interpreted each glance he gave her with cool psychoanalysis. *Such a kind man to help his father out on the farm when he has free time*, she thought. Her daydreaming was rudely interrupted by the chorus of the hounds outside. They both walked out to the gate, curious about another visitor. Cowering, her mind suddenly returned, telling her in a pathetic whine that she had forgotten about her sister. Tiffany stood with her arms folded; her face stony and unphased by the raucous tide of barking around her. Her gaze was firm and held Paige's. "Forget something, Paige?"

"I'm sorry Tiff, I got a bit distracted."

"It's my fault really." The voice startled Tiffany as she realised that someone else was present. Her face fell.

"Andrew?"

"Hello again, Tiffany, I didn't expect to see you so soon."

"You two know each other?" asked Paige.

"We met each other last night at the bar." Paige fell silent, her mind's dreaming shattered.

"Looks like you two girls could do with some help. Get back to your car and I'll follow in a few minutes to see if I can help get you going again."

The sisters walked in silence, neither dared to look in the other's direction. Each feeling rejected and stupid for thinking that a man would want them as something more than a friend. But this soon faded and both felt bitter resentment for each other for stopping the dreams that made them happy, even if it was for the briefest moment. As they waited for Andrew they sat on opposite banks of the road, an argument looming like a dark cloud over the horizon. Pride is such a fickle trait. It didn't take long for Andy to refill their tank, nor did it take him long to realise that the pair weren't talking.

"I hope you two girls weren't arguing over me?" The silence from each of them was enough, but the blushes that spread on their cheeks finalised the answer to his question. "Well, ladies I'm flattered. Truly I am. But if you're going to argue over me, at least speak to my wife about it first."

The Old Wife's Tale

Rosie Canning

"An housbonde shal nat been inquisityf

Of Goddes pryvetee, nor of his wyf.

So he may fynde Goddes foyson there,

Of the remenant nedeth nat enquere."

The Miller's Prologue

Jeremy Bath was desperate and confused. There was only a week and a day left before the presentation. Facts and figures, figures and facts; his head was swimming.

"What's the matter Jeremy, why do you keep looking at your watch?" Queen Bee, Maggie Schmitt, Head of Psychology at York University, stared at him.

"I'm going to be late for work," he said, but that wasn't the real reason. He'd been trying not to stare at the red lace bra peeping over the top of her low-cut dress.

"So what do you do when you're not studying?" she asked.

"I'm a motorbike courier." She raised her black-pencilled eyebrows. Jeremy was used to that sort of reaction when mentioning his job. He thought it was the thick glasses that made him seem all bumbly; not at all like a crazy biker screaming into the night, the wind slapping against his face. But inside lurked a powerful man, a man who gathered protesting women in his arms. He dreamt of women often – even Maggie Schmitt – slung over a desk, skirt raised…

"You've missed the point, Jeremy." Maggie Schmitt looked up from the thick pile of research papers. "You've got some interesting ideas, but you haven't convinced me that you've got to the heart of what it is that women really want." She smiled; a crack of a smile that stayed in her mouth.

Jeremy pleaded, "Can't you be more specific? Can't you just tell me what's missing?"

She tapped a pen on the desk, "I'm not here to do the work for you. You've had nearly a year, it should be finished by now." She handed him the papers. "This is your last chance. Mess this up and you're out, off the course."

Failure for Jeremy was a sentence worse than death. Death when it finally came was swift; failure was like a barnacle attaching itself to a shell, cemented and perpetual. Tiny specks of rain, like needles, tapped against the window. The Psychology Department, with its distinctive chequer-board rotunda, overlooked a large lake surrounded by weeping willows. He watched as a man, dressed in a raincoat, threw a stick into the water. A small furry dog chased after it and, clutching it in its mouth, paddled like crazy to stay afloat.

"The only thing I can suggest," said Maggie, putting a red line through Jeremy's name, "Is that you interview a few more women; preferably older than twenty-five!" There was a knock at the door. "Come in!"

Jeremy gathered his papers; some fell to the floor, Maggie sighed. He headed towards the door. "Good luck," she said.

The rain, now lashing down, made vision difficult. Jeremy's motorbike drowned out the hum of slow-moving traffic. At this time of day, it was better to go to the Theatre Royal via Nunnery Lane, rather than up Tower Street, where the roads would be packed with wandering tourists. Sometimes, if he had time to spare, he liked to walk round the city, even treat himself to one of the sights. Jeremy raced towards the lights, screeching to a halt as they turned red. His favourite was the Castle Museum, especially on a hot day. When exploring the old prisons he often found himself drawn to the condemned cell. Standing against a cold brick wall, he imagined himself as the notorious, flamboyant Dick Turpin, waiting fearlessly in the dark before being hanged. With a flick of the throttle, he sped past the station towards Lendal Bridge; in the distance he could see the theatre.

Jeremy came in from the rain, through a stage door at the side of the theatre. Removing his helmet, he nodded at the doorman, "Package for Jenny Eccles." He brushed the water from his leathers.

"Up there," the doorman indicated a short flight of stairs. "See the stage manager, he'll know where Jenny is."

Looking at the parcel, Jeremy remembered another Jenny, Jenny Atkinson. Just the name made him shiver. Jenny. It had all been so wonderful when it began. Teenage sweethearts: Jenny and Jeremy – perfect. Two leading lights in the Bletchley Park Amateur Dramatic Society. Jenny was a born actress and beautiful too. Two magical summers. They were madly in love. He even imagined they'd get married one day. That was until her seventeenth birthday. He wanted to make it oh so special. He took her to a French restaurant. She had veal and he had steak tartare and, of course, a bottle of champagne. They stopped at the cemetery on the way home. It was a warm and balmy evening. Jenny took off her cardigan, folding it into a makeshift pillow, and laid down amidst the buttercups. She unbuttoned the top three buttons on her dress. It was obvious; at last she was ready. It was amazing making love with Jenny that night; at least it had been, until 1.45 the next afternoon when he rang and her mother answered. "You've got a nerve ringing here. Jenny doesn't want to speak to you." The line went dead. Instantly his world shattered. She didn't even reply to his letters. Some weeks later he overheard some girls whispering at a bus stop. He heard Jenny's name and the word 'rape'; he put two and two together. After that, Jeremy vowed never to marry. Women, he had decided, could eat you up and spit you out like a pip, like a sour, bitter pip.

Jeremy found himself backstage. Ahead was a wondrous sight, he couldn't believe his luck; it quite took his breath away. A group of semi-naked nymphs were dancing round an old woman, an old hag of a woman.

A man banged a clipboard. "Great." He looked at his watch. "Tea time."

One by one the nymphs floated off the stage. The old hag stood up, rubbing her back and stretching her arms in the air. Jeremy ran over to the man with the clipboard. "Parcel for Jenny Eccles."

"That's Jenny," he pointed at the old woman. She smiled and walked towards them.

Jeremy handed her the parcel.

She studied him. "Don't I know you?"

"I don't think so." Jeremy felt uncomfortable under her gaze.

"Shouldn't I sign something?"

He nodded, pulling a piece of paper from inside his leather jacket.

"Follow me," she said, marching across the stage.

"I've got a pen here!" he shouted after her, but she ignored him.

He followed her round the back of the stage, past a girl in overalls painting scenery, and a group of young lads lifting a large canvas. Jeremy had an idea. Maybe this Jenny Eccles could help. She looked at least seventy, an actress, must have been around a bit in her youth. He would ask her.

She disappeared through a doorway. The room was full of brightly coloured outfits. Photos of actors and actresses, some in colour, some in black and white, adorned the walls. Jenny picked up a pen from a dressing table, and signed the form. "Here we are." She handed it back.

He coughed. Women in the flesh always made him nervous. He coughed again. "I was wondering, perhaps you, ermm…"

"Do you want my autograph?" Her stony eyes widened. Her face was ravaged by old age, wrinkled, and caked in orange make-up, and her crooked nose had a large bump on the ridge. The hair was grey, it looked like a wig; God she was ugly.

"The thing is…"

"Oh for God's sake spit it out."

"I'm doing a presentation next week at the University. The theme is 'Relationships and Sexuality in the Twenty-First Century', it's part of my research. I know what men want," he smiled, but she didn't smile back. "But when it comes to women," he shrugged his shoulders, "I've questioned over one hundred of them in the last year, but they all seem to want something different. Some want financial security, some want fun in bed, some want separate houses, and some just want to be pampered and flattered. I'm totally confused and if I don't work it out, I'm a dead man. Do you know what women *really* want in a relationship?"

She laughed. "Of course I do, but don't you have a pretty young wife to help you?"

Jeremy shook his head. "I'll never marry."

"Why?"

He was silent.

"Supposing I help you," she said. "What do I get in return?"

"I'd do anything, I'm desperate. Trim the hedge, sweep the path, fix things, anything."

"Anything?" Walking towards the door, she added, "You promise?"

Jeremy nodded.

Closing the door, she pointed to a chair and smiled, "So you'd marry me then?"

He giggled, "Of course." He was beginning to relax.

Jeremy was tongue-tied. The more he tried, the more the words got stuck in his mouth and only bits of them wiggled out. He'd lost his place. Hundreds of staring eyes waited. Maggie Schmitt, sitting next to the Dean, smiled – one of her impatient smiles. He recovered himself; the spidery scribble in front of him became clear. "What makes women happy?" He sounded authoritative. "What do women really want in a relationship?" He looked at Maggie. "A woman wants to be king and queen over her lover, her partner, her mate. Woe betide the man or woman who tries to dominate her.

Sovereignty and control; that, ladies and gentlemen, is what women want." He paused, "Thank you."

For a moment there was silence. Then suddenly clapping and roars of approval filled the hall. Most of the women were standing and cheering. Maggie Schmitt walked onto the stage.

She whispered, "Looks like you're off the hook." Speaking into the microphone, she began, "Quiet now." The noise subsided. "Well done, Jeremy." Turning back to the audience she asked, "Any questions?"

A woman shouted: "If a man makes a promise, do you think he should honour it?"

"I most certainly do," Jeremy looked towards the back of the hall in the direction of the voice. It was the old hag from the theatre. What was she doing here? A few heads turned.

"You promised to do anything if I helped you. I asked you to marry me and you said yes." There was a splatter of giggles from the audience. "Remember?"

"Well?" said Maggie Schmitt. "Did you promise to marry this woman?"

Jeremy looked at his tutor and back at the old woman. "Well, it was a joke. I didn't mean it."

"My car's outside," shouted the old woman. "It'll only take us a couple of hours to get to Gretna Green."

The audience began to chant: "Je-re-my, Je-re-my."

"A promise is a promise," said Maggie. "You'll have to go."

It was a joke. The old bag wouldn't go through with it. Jeremy laughed and waved at the audience. He was getting into the spirit of it. By the door, he held out his arm. The old woman curtseyed and took it. They left the hall together.

They lay side by side in The Honeymoon Hotel, very near to the registry office. In one of the corners of the room, there was a patch of damp on the pink-flowered wallpaper. The smell of cheap air-freshener made Jeremy's nose tingle.

"Shall I turn off the light?" asked Jenny.

He ignored her. The room was plunged into darkness. Her face brushed against his. He felt sick; she was all rubbery and wrinkly. She pulled at his trousers. "Enough," he cried, leaping up from the bed.

"What is it, what's the matter?"

"I can't," he said, "I can't do it." He couldn't see her face properly in the dark, but it was etched into his memory. "You're too old." He sneezed three times.

Laughing, she switched the light back on. "Now you listen to me young man, I saved your bacon. Anyway, I've got a good figure for my age." She pulled up her nightdress, "Look at my legs." Jeremy closed his eyes. "Just imagine this," she moved towards him. "I could stay like this," snuggling up, she rested her cheek against his chest. "Old. You would always be confident of my faithfulness and love for you." He moved away. "Or I could become a beautiful, young woman with many admirers," she flung her arms in the air and pirouetted. "You might become jealous, not sure of my faithfulness." She cackled like a witch. "Think carefully. Which would you prefer?"

Jeremy sat in a chair at the end of the bed. He was tired. "You decide," he said.

"Right answer," said the old woman. She ran into the bathroom and locked the door.

When she came out Jeremy was startled. He grabbed his glasses from the bedside locker; before him was not an old woman, but a nymph-like creature with long, dark hair. He recognised her, older yes, but it was..."Jenny Atkinson," he said.

"The wife of Jeremy Bath now." And now he recognised her voice.

Taking his hand she led him into the bathroom. A grey wig sat perched on the corner of the bath. She pointed to bits of a pink, rubbery material that lay in the sink. "Make-up. You're so short-sighted you didn't even notice. Eccles is my stage name. I often used to wonder what happened to you, and then a few months ago I heard you were doing a PhD at York." For a moment there was silence. "I'm so sorry about what happened, it was my mother. She found the contraceptives in my bag and went bonkers. She wouldn't let me out of the house for weeks – I nearly died of shame." She wrapped herself around him, "Forgive me?"

The Trainer's Tale

David Darton

"A man moot nedes love…"

The Knight's Tale

Peter came to York to go to University. He loved it. After his stultifying, aspiring, lower-middle-class upbringing in a small Home Counties town (his way of describing it once he was into his politics degree), he found freedom. He got into a liberal, fun-loving, bohemian crowd where, for the first time, he could try things out and discover things about himself. He could be exploratory in a place where experimentation was the norm, not something for small town bigots to make snide comments about.

You could create your own world on the university campus, never having to venture into the city, except for the odd pub crawl. Everyone, of course, had to try the Micklegate Run – a drink in every pub and bar down Micklegate until you arrive at Ouse Bridge to be sick, a dozen or more drinks the worse for wear. But that was okay for first-year students, young army recruits from the surrounding camps, young men in dead-end jobs, secretaries looking to make an aspirational catch and women out for a 'night with the girls and the odd man if you could catch him'. This is where Peter lost his virginity, with great relief, in an alley near the river, and met, in the bars and clubs of this fair city, a series of temporary lovers. At the end of three years, he graduated with a 2-2 in politics and the world was his oyster.

Well not quite. Have you ever tried to get a job with a politics degree? Or get full funding for a higher degree when you don't have a 'first'? Peter needed at least a year of work at a reasonable salary. But he was over-qualified for most jobs and under-qualified for the few that came with decent money.

And then came his saviour. A huge, new health club, gym and swimming pool complex had just been built in Fulford, not far from the University. And it needed staff.

Peter had always been quite narcissistic. Flexing his body in front of the mirror at least once a day for as long as he could remember. At Uni he had been able to indulge himself at the highly-subsidised sporting facilities. As his muscles developed, the flexing began to feed his pride, rather than lower his esteem. Not only did he get employed as a fitness instructor, but as *chief* fitness instructor, no less. They assumed his university career would enable him to do the admin work this required.

Now, more than a year later, life felt good. He was in a proper long-term relationship for the first time. Although he occasionally had doubts about whether this was right for him, they had moved in together. So far no major problems and he guessed he might actually be in love. The money wasn't brilliant, but he had stopped pursuing anything else. He enjoyed his work and often assigned himself to cover vacant shifts, rather than forcing them on his staff.

One particular afternoon, Peter turned to another of the instructors, a large powerfully-built young black lad from the Midlands, "I've really been looking forward to this, Daniel," he said. "I've got Sally for my next session. That's why I changed my shift at the last moment. She's really hot for me, you know, and keeps making passes."

Sally and he had been indulging in ever-more adventurous flirtation for a while. No actual contact. Nothing to be ashamed of. But, he thought, maybe this afternoon he could be persuaded by Sally to go further. There was something about all the physical exertion around in this place that heightened these things as effectively as the Micklegate alcohol. And maybe it would help him decide if he really should be living with his lover, or still playing the field and experimenting, like most of his contemporaries. Although things at home had been reasonably blissful recently, he still felt a little unsettled. He needed to know where his true loyalties lay.

He might even get to use the shag hole for the first time. The shag hole was a large unused storeroom that the male trainers had designated, during one drunken bonding session, the place for a 'quick one', should the opportunity arise. And Peter knew of two definite uses of it already. Well, it is difficult to stop guys boasting. In strictest confidence, of course.

"Anyway, I had better go and spruce myself up for," he paused suggestively, "the session." Peter found himself enjoying the sensation of macho bravado.

Daniel raised his eyebrows and grinned at the expression spreading across Peter's face. Daniel might be gay, but it didn't stop him appreciating sexual anticipation, even in straights. And was it a pang of jealousy he also felt? He liked Peter a lot, but of course he would never admit to being gay in the testosterone-fuelled atmosphere of the gym and locker room. Anyway, he was practiced at disguising it, helped by his build and race, which meant that the stereotypes people applied to him never included 'gay'.

Daniel was brought up in a rough neighbourhood. A failing school and decaying slums. Half-abandoned tower blocks in the run-down estates to the north-west of Birmingham. He survived the gangs because he was always big and mean-looking for his age. Daniel was the slightly weird, but tough loner, who was useful as a mediator when the need arose.

The first inkling he had that he was gay, was when he 'messed around' with a friend a year older than him. The friend moved onto girls. Daniel gradually realized he wasn't going to move on. And that meant that he had to move out. How would a goddamn queer survive on his streets? So he joined the army.

Biggest mistake ever. The racism at the camp he was at outside York was barely under the surface. But he survived. Being only seventeen, he had a get-out at eighteen and, luckily, didn't have to do a full three years. Now here he was in a great job. He could safely go to the gay bars in nearby Leeds. The all-night train journey to Leeds and Manchester meant nothing had developed here in York – probably much to the relief of conservative North Yorkshire. So in York, and especially at the health club, Daniel disciplined himself not to hit on any of the punters. It wasn't really fair though, he thought, as Peter went off to meet Sally. He would never get to use the shag hole. And he knew there were opportunities. Not all the mutual examination in the male locker room was innocent comparison of muscle tone.

He suddenly found himself feeling very horny, and even a little reckless, as he thought of Peter getting his end away – even if it was with a woman. Anyway, he had his next appointment coming up and that would take his mind off it. A first-timer. He looked at the card in his hand. Brian. He was late. Maybe he wasn't going to turn up. The good intentions sometimes failed at the last hurdle, especially among the club's main clients: middle-aged, middle-class people who were better at guilt, than at action.

Peter felt competitively good as he sensed Daniel's jealousy. He wondered if he would actually go through with it if Sally gave him the come-on. His casual relationships with women were usually fairly disastrous. And it would be a big betrayal. But for some reason he wanted to feel as much of a lad as the rest of his staff and, for once, share properly in their bravado and banter. After all, he was only twenty-three.

Peter had arranged to meet Sally on one of the higher balconies for warm-up stretches. The club was quite sprawling, with three floors, plus balconies at half-floor levels and a complex array of staircases on three of the four sides of the central area. The central area itself had been divided on two of the floors into different equipment rooms and studios for aerobics and Alexander Technique and Pilates and Yoga and all the various fads of inner muscle control that were, and still are, so fashionable.

Peter couldn't help an involuntary gasp as Sally rose into view, gliding up the stairs. She was wearing a skin-coloured leotard and tights that clung to everything except her long luxurious black hair. For a split second Peter thought that she was a naked Egyptian goddess. In this moment he was surprised at the strength of the reaction in his manhood to this dark, slim, sensuous woman. She was such a complete opposite to what he was building his life around at home. Sally smiled at him in that seductive, half-questioning way she had. Yes, she was definitely gagging for it.

After a while of stretching, she started to complain about the strain on her breasts; that maybe they needed supporting better, if he knew what she meant. It wasn't actually her breasts that were causing the reaction in Peter. It was her never-ending legs, toned in a way that he knew would grip him just where he needed it.

He brought his mind back to what she was saying. It was definitely a come-on. She had developed good pectoral muscles over the last few weeks and certainly didn't need any extra support. But he said, "We've got some products that might help – in one of our store rooms. We can go there just before the end of the session." He couldn't believe he had just said that. He momentarily felt nervous as he remembered past failures at casual sex. But the smile he got to his offer was radiant. Much to his surprise he found himself getting turned-on even more, without feeling any guilt. He made a mental note to go to the front desk and arrange for one of the other trainers to take his next client so that he would not be rushed, assuming all went to plan.

If Peter's heart was missing a beat or two, so too was Daniel's. Brian, rushing in late, had turned out to be drop-dead gorgeous. Maybe just this once, Daniel thought. He just knew with this one. There was something about Brian's eyelashes and the way he had his bleached-blonde hair styled. He was talking continuously and breathlessly, in that way a certain type of gay person does. And it was the type Daniel liked. Over the last year in the Leeds clubs, he had found out what really turned him on. It was being the dominant one with pale-skinned, and preferably blonde, guys. This was probably because it was the only time that he felt that he was the one in control. Some white guys had fetishes about being taken by black men and on these occasions his dark skin was actually desired. It was the only time he felt his colour was positive and something to flaunt. Most of the time, in virtually all-white North Yorkshire, Daniel felt, in Peter's words, 'the weight of historical oppression'. Only in sex did that go away completely, though somewhere in his mind Daniel knew that this wasn't enough. He knew he wouldn't settle for a life of casual shags, like some he had met. But in the meantime, why not?

After going through the paperwork and the conditions of membership with Brian, Daniel was hooked, especially when Brian's hand brushed his own in a lingering fashion as he handed him the pen. Daniel decided that he would make this session run over slightly. If he was going to use the shag hole, he needed to be sure that Peter was finished and that he had another client straight after Sally.

Daniel took Brian to one of the quieter balconies upstairs to show him the stretching exercises. With luck, it would be empty at this time of day and he could linger a little in helping Brian work out the stretches. Brian was fussing over the beginning of a love handle and said that he had promised... he paused. Well, promised himself, to work at getting rid of it. Daniel smiled inwardly. He wondered what lucky man Brian had promised. He hoped it didn't preclude some extra-curricular cardio-vascular work to get the heart going.

"Stretching," Daniel explained, as he led Brian on to the mat-covered balcony, "is essential for treadmill and cross-training work to be effective." He saw Sally's distinctive hair disappearing down the stairs on the opposite side. It reminded him that Peter might be getting his way soon. The thought made him twitch you-know-where and made him more determined than ever that, just this once, he would have some relief during the day.

Peter led Sally down the stairs. "I just need to check something out at the front desk," he said, "go on into the free weights room and we'll do some upper body work."

Sally was stretched out on the bench when he came into the room, her endless legs an open invitation, her head back under the weight bar with her eyes shut and her long, dark hair spilling onto the floor. Peter walked very quietly round her, but Sally sensed his presence and, as though stretching by accident, reached up and touched him gently on the face. Both drew breath sharply, the sparks flying between them. She didn't open her eyes, as would have been the innocent response. Peter looked around. The room was momentarily empty. He bent down, not sure what to say. But Sally raised her head slightly and brushed her lips from his neck, to his ear. The surprise of it pressed all his buttons at once. He whispered that they had better do some weights. First.

"First?" Sally murmured. "What did you think might come next?" Peter was saved from answering, as some others came noisily into the room and he became all business.

Daniel was all business too, taking Brian through the beginners' routine. He took every opportunity to steady Brian when he was doing stretches that involved balancing on one leg. It was going well. At one point, as he steadied Brian, Daniel said, "Of course you can use a wall when you are on your own." Much to his delight, as he was holding him a little longer than strictly necessary, he received the reply, "but it wouldn't be nearly as much fun," accompanied by a long, direct gaze from Brian's bright blue eyes.

However, as you know, there is a difference between what was becoming increasingly obvious flirting and actually getting down to it. Daniel would need an excuse to get Brian into the shag hole, even though Brian was now hanging onto his every word and looking at him increasingly like a puppy beholding his master. Daniel decided that he would have to arrange a small 'strain' for Brian and then take him to the 'first aid room' (otherwise known as the shag hole).

As they entered the free-weights room, he again saw Sally leaving by the far door, presumably being led by Peter. Daniel checked his watch. Peter wasn't leaving himself much time, maybe he wasn't going to get his way after all. Daniel couldn't help feeling pleased. Mind you, he had better make sure that it was well into the next session before he took Brian for some 'first aid'.

Daniel led Brian into a side room and spent time with him on the fixed-weight machines until the hour session officially ended. Then he brought him back into the free-weights room.

"I don't normally introduce free-weights to people at the beginning, but," thinking flattery would do his cause no harm, "your body is in such good shape really."

"Not like your body, though, is it?" giggled Brian, running his eyes more slowly than necessary up and down Daniel's body, pausing where an impatient part of Daniel's anatomy was now making itself felt.

"Well, these weights will help," Daniel said, after an extended silence. "Here, get down on the bench and we'll try a simple chest press." Brian lay on his back and Daniel positioned Brian's arms by his side, bent at the elbow so that his hands were raised above his chest. He then took a weight bar from the rack and lowered it from above, towards Brian's up-turned hands. Just before the bar came to rest in Brian's hands, Daniel dropped one end, pushing it with a little force in a way that he knew would send a shock down the arm to Brian's elbow. Brian screeched, bringing looks from the two women exercising down at the other end of the room. Daniel raised the bar quickly and apologized.

"Come on, better get that looked at in our first aid room." Daniel said, although he knew that within a minute or so the tingling pain would go. Brian meekly followed him, nursing his elbow.

There was no light coming from under the door. Good. Peter must have finished or not got to first base. Daniel was never sure afterwards why he assumed that they would have the light on.

He checked up and down the dimly lit corridor, which was fortunately empty as usual. "This is just a place to recover quietly from light injury," he explained, as he turned the handle and went in. His hand went to the light switch and, behold, a tableaux was lit as if by spotlight on a stage. Peter, with trousers around his ankles, being serviced by a wildly bobbing head of long black hair.

Sally was moving frantically in a last effort, because Peter was not responding in the flesh as he had fondly imagined he would in the anticipation. The next few moments were not going to help.

Before Daniel could get an apology out and beat a hasty retreat, there was a scream from behind him and Brian's voice rose an octave higher than his normal, already high pitch.

"Peter! Oh, how could you? Oh, you absolute bitch. Oh God. And it's a woman." He pushed past an astounded Daniel, who had the presence of mind to close the door. Brian stood for a moment, hand on hip, and then flounced purposefully towards Peter and slapped him hard across the face.

Sally scrambled back from Peter, leaving him in not very much glory. "What's going on?" Sally demanded of Peter, turning ever-deeper shades of red as she struggled back into her tight leotard.

"What's going on?" screeched Brian. "What's going on? You mean you don't know what you were doing? It's got several names you know. Not that you were doing it very well. Going at it like an express train. When I do it to him, nice and slow, he has a very different reaction I can tell you."

Sally's eyes looked like they were going to pop out of her head. "You mean, you…" She looked at Peter, "Jesus, you're… Oh. Oh my god." Suddenly she was up. Pushing past Daniel, she flung open the door, slammed it behind her and was gone.

Peter was rubbing his cheek. Brian started screeching again. "You bastard. You complete bastard," and slapped the other side of his face. Peter came out of his trance and grabbed Brian's hands. "It wasn't anything. You see. Well you saw. I couldn't…"

"You betrayed me, you bastard. You bastard." Brian began sobbing hysterically.

"Anyway, what are you doing here?" asked Peter, in a forlorn attempt to regain some composure – difficult with Brian struggling in his arms and his trousers still around his ankles.

"What am I doing here? What am I doing here? I'm supposed to be recuperating after a nasty little accident." Peter looked across at Daniel, who shrugged helplessly. "An injury to my arm," Brian continued through sobs, "got, I might add, because I promised you the other night – you know when we were, when we were… and I couldn't keep going – that I would try and be as fit as you are. It was going to be a surprise, me joining your precious club," he wailed. "Anyway, what are you doing here? It was meant to be your day off."

"I had to do… emergency cover." His eyes pleaded with Daniel. God, he couldn't believe all this was happening in front of Daniel. By tomorrow he would be a laughing stock. He was finished as a fitness instructor here – and after all the trouble he had taken to keep being gay secret.

"Darling, I do love you," Peter said pleadingly. "I didn't…" Brian pulled away.

"Don't you 'darling' me. You cad. I want you out." If it was possible, Brian's voice rose another half octave. "Out. Do you hear? Don't you dare come home tonight. Don't come anywhere near me again. You…You…You, closet straight!"

And with that the show ended. Brian stood up. Straightened his hair, drew his shoulders up and his chest in and, rather than flouncing in his usual way, marched with some dignity from the room.

Daniel sensibly decided it was politic to leave too.

Peter took the next day off, phoning in sick. He tried to explain things to Brian. That he just needed to see if he could be with a woman. That he wasn't really settled, even though he thought he loved Brian. Brian was having none of it and eventually Peter got angry. After all, Brian, despite his denials, was obviously going to try and seduce Daniel, even though he was straight.

The following day Peter went to the gym full of trepidation, anxiously awaiting the smirks of the other trainers and perhaps even an embarrassing exchange with the Centre Manager, on why it might be better if Peter left. But there was nothing. No smirks. No calls to the manager's office. Daniel hadn't told. Yet.

It took a week for Peter to risk an embarrassed word with Daniel and discover why his secret would remain a secret.

A month later Daniel and Peter made love for the first time. For the first time, Peter did not try and perform the male dominant role. He let go of the idea that his masculinity was dependent on his sexual preferences. And Daniel made love vigorously because he wanted to please both of them, not because he needed someone else's desire to affirm his value as a human being.

A year later, they were living together. Peter didn't *probably* love Daniel. He *definitely* loved him, and his heart whooped every time he thought it. He knew that they were young and he couldn't be certain that it would last. But it was good and it was possible because he had something else that he knew *would* stay forever. Love of himself.

A Very Blue Tale

Polly Redman

"And therfore every man this tale I telle

Wynne who so may, for al is for to selle;

With empty hand men may none haukes lure;

For wynnyng wolde I al his lust endure..."

The Wife of Bath's Tale

It was there, just as he had said. Chained to the drainpipe, the blue bicycle looked quaint and forlorn. It was an original way to dress a restaurant entrance. The front wheel was proudly pointing to the doorway. He had told her that it would be there as long as it hadn't been pinched. Over the years, the bicycle had become renowned for being stolen. After glancing at its sky-blue frame, she couldn't help but wonder why someone would want to steal it –the saddle looked pretty stiff and worn for comfortable mounting. She quickly concluded that its theft must have been the result of a dare rather than desire. Blue was her favourite colour. Seeing the bicycle was a pleasant start to the evening. Tonight her husband was away again on one of his business trips, but Jenny would be here, dining for the first time with one of his best friends.

Walking towards the doorway, she spotted a picture of one of the girls that had worked there a long time ago, proudly displayed in the window. Not many places would boast that their premises used to be a brothel, but the Blue Bicycle restaurant positively advertised the fact. Surrounded by pretty flower baskets, the woman that had once prostituted herself here was now offered as a display of femininity. How history had changed things! The aged picture of her with a feather boa provocatively draped over her bare breasts reminded Jenny to thank God for the inventor of the Wonder Bra. Without it, she knew that she would certainly not be displaying the voluptuous cleavage that was on show tonight.

The glamorous and sexy feeling she'd experienced after donning that essential item of lingerie and a stylish, body-hugging little black dress, seemed to vanish as the smell of fish greeted her. Any remaining traces evaporated as she struggled to follow the waiter down the winding staircase. Its curved frame seemed to ridicule her with its cold, wry grin. She had never been able to walk in high heels, and tonight wasn't any different. Through the long French windows, Jenny could see the River Foss flowing alongside the restaurant. Struggling to make the elegant entrance that she so wanted to make, she envied the way in which the river flowed so powerfully, but so effortlessly. More pictures of the girls who used to work there adorned the cellar walls. Their eyes followed her, willing her onwards and downwards and into the warm cellar where he was waiting. The girls' spirits tittered as they glared at Damien watching Jenny descending the stairs and walking towards him. He relished every movement that she made. The ghosts that loitered could smell his lust, just as pungently as Jenny could smell the salmon speciality of the house.

Millie and Betsy had both been women that knew how to please a man. Their knowledge had been so extensive that men would come from near and far to pay them for pleasure. Countless customers had looked at them in the way that Damien was looking at Jenny. That was a long time ago, now they had left their bodies behind and operated in another realm. Being able to see beyond flesh and blood, Millie and Betsy drifted unseen, hovering among the shadows. The nude pictures that hung in the cellar were posted in faded black and white, but their spirits hadn't faded over the years. They were still colourful and mischievous. Amusing themselves by flitting between the tables, they would linger within the dimness, listening silently as the diners engaged each other in conversation. Betsy liked to listen to the groups of businessmen that would often eat there. Their conversation was a dance of words, as they skilfully choreographed the truth in order to please and entertain their associates. It reminded her of the past and the way in which she had done this with her customers so many years ago. Seeing beyond the physical realm afforded its own kind of entertainment. To these spirits, Damien was not just a man, but a mixture of many things. As they looked into his soul, he could not hide his cravings and desires from them.

Damien and Jenny were sat in the booth that had held Millie's bed, so long ago. Damien's hands reminded her of the first man she had serviced here. Millie had been unprepared for such smooth hands to treat her so roughly. She had only serviced this gentleman once as he always asked for a virgin, in the belief that familiarity with a virgin would cure his venereal disease. She soon discovered that intimacy with the innocent could never cure the guilty. Afterwards Millie had felt tainted and soiled. Betsy had told her that the first time would be the worst, she had been right. When he grunted as he pushed his body against hers, she felt as if a filthy stain had blotted her soul. She knew that her body and soul weren't like the bedclothes that could be scrubbed spotless and starched to look new again, but in some way, being able to send money home to her family made her feel clean – if only for the moment it took to seal the envelope. Millie told her mother and sisters that she was employed in the squire's domestic service. It wasn't a complete lie, just a little alteration of the facts; after all, she did work for the squire. She was his whore.

Cocooned in the small booth, Jenny looked around the room, curiously admiring the unusual surroundings. The dim, fluted table light emitted a glow that bounced off the red textured walls, making them glisten as if the paint was still wet and new. Jenny envied the nude woman in the picture on the wall; her body seemed to curve in all the right places without being assisted by any lingerie. The décor seemed a sophisticated celebration of the softness and curvatures of the female body. A solid wooden beam stood out from the wall, serving as a shelf above the fireplace. On the shelf stood an old wooden clock, a few pictures and some books.

This restaurant was warm and inviting. It was here that Millie and Betsy were now sentenced to see, but not be seen. The voices that had laughed and made merry in the brothel were now a mere whisper, only heard by those who would abandon reason and yield to the demands of passionate desire. No longer able to enjoy the sensual dimension of the physical realm, Millie and Betsy had to satisfy themselves by watching the gratification of others. Damien had fostered a desire for Jenny's body for a long time now; if that craving were to reach fulfilment this evening, Millie and Betsy would be able to relish the pleasure of his satisfaction. Unheard, Millie began to whisper in Jenny's ear, waiting and hoping that when the moment of temptation came, Jenny would embrace it fully.

Damien interrupted Jenny's thoughts, "What's on the menu?" he asked. His question seemed straightforward, but his tone of voice was playful, hinting at something more. As Millie looked on unseen, she understood what he was asking. He wanted to know if Jenny wanted him in the way that he wanted her. The menu offered little choice for Jenny, she hated fish and much of the menu was taken up with seafood dishes. Perhaps this was an omen for her. A sign that tonight could be a disaster.

Had she been with her husband, Jenny would have expressed her concerns at the cost of the food, but not with Damien. Damien always seemed to have more than enough money. He wasn't deliberately elusive about his occupation, but Jenny found it difficult to identify exactly what he did that seemed to be so successful. Despite his frequent explanations of the rudiments of the stock market, she could never fully grasp them. Tonight he wanted to mark the occasion of an unexpected, huge return from a small investment. On his sound advice, several of his clients had profited, ensuring his promotion. Adding to the good news was the fact that he had been shrewd enough to buy a large amount of these shares with his own money. Yesterday, he had sold them and they had proved more lucrative than even he could have predicted. A single man with no wife or current girlfriend, Damien would normally have celebrated these events with his drinking partner, Jenny's husband, Peter. Damien was delighted at the prospect of being able to buy a new car. With Peter he would have discussed the car's specifications, its engine capacity, its in-car sound system and its ergonomic design; along with so many other exciting particulars. As a woman, he felt that Jenny was not really able to appreciate these precise details. So he translated his explicit description into one that made it simple for her. He told her that he would be buying an open-top sports car.

Despite her own financial hardship, her sweet nature couldn't help but be pleased at his good fortune. Whilst talking with Jenny, his eyes skimmed up and down her body. His excitement was no longer caused by the impending acquisition of a vehicle, but by her proximity. Rather than being disappointed by the absence of Peter, his whole body was stimulated by the presence of Jenny. Peter was elsewhere, devoting his time to a business venture that he had promised his wife might be the answer to all their money worries. That's what he always said.

Although expensive, the food was good and they both enjoyed the meal. Jenny's face flushed as she drank the fruity wine and it loosened her inhibitions. Damien began to tell her how alluring she was. Going beyond his usual compliments, he told her he longed to be able to touch her body; that he would love to spend the whole night with her, not just the evening. Another time or place and she would have been embarrassed by his confessions, but here she dared to enjoy them. Jenny began to take pleasure in his attention and could feel the excitement stirring in her. Millie and Betsy's whisperings became murmurings in her head, filling her soul with suggestion. The restless spirits had now found a place to settle. Spurred on by her need, their whisperings gave her the confidence that she had lacked. She fixed her eyes on Damien, captivating him

"How much do you want me Damien, how much is a night with me worth to you?" She was amazed to hear him tell her that she was worth at least three thousand pounds, maybe even four. Some women may have found his advances insulting, but Jenny desperately needed that kind of money. Money was the real reason for her accepting his invitation to dine this evening. The most she had hoped for was a loan, but this was beyond anything she had anticipated.

"I'm sure," she said firmly, disguising her nervousness, "I'm sure I can be worth four thousand pounds." Millie and Betsy laughed impishly, knowing that Jenny would look back on tonight and wonder what had possessed her to be so bold. Damien's response was no surprise, after all, he was trained to recognise a good investment and he knew how to close a deal.

The ghostly pursuit of entertainment had yielded its rewards for the enterprising spirits. Betsy wished she could follow Damien and Jenny as they left, but Millie was more than satisfied with the amusement that they had already provided. Damien discreetly enquired as to the availability of the Blue Rooms, the apartments behind the restaurant. He wasn't disappointed.

In contrast to the stone floor of the Blue Bicycle, the apartment had a plush carpet. Her bare feet sank into its deep pile as she undressed slowly, while he gazed at her. She needn't have been concerned that he would be disappointed. She climbed into the huge four-poster bed that was draped with white linen and he eagerly climbed in next to her. Touching her without restraint, he struggled to contain himself. She felt the warmth of his body and the dampness of his mouth pressed against hers and had a sudden terrible thought. What would her mother say? Was she selling her soul? But when he held her face and passionately kissed her, she pushed these thoughts out of her mind. As he indulged himself in this body that he had longed to feel against his, she resisted her conscience and surrendered to the moment. Something so bad couldn't possibly feel so good. As if knowing her thoughts, he spoke quietly. "Did you know that the human body has no straight lines? There are no absolutes, no certainties, only this moment." At that instant she decided that she would put his cheque in her bank account on the way home, tomorrow morning.

Arriving home she took off her shoes in the hallway and could see that the answer phone was flashing. She hadn't expected Peter to call. He usually tried to avoid the cost of phone calls when he was abroad. She wasn't in a hurry to hear his voice this morning. Anyway, she didn't have time. She had just banked the cheque that Damien had given her, the money needed to be in her account as soon as possible. Now it was time to pack her bags. She was going away for a week, on a trip she had planned some time ago. Thanks to Damien, she now had the money to do exactly what she had intended. Over time, she'd managed to filter money from her and Peter's joint bank account without him noticing. She had got as far as paying the deposit for her little adventure. Until last night, finding the balance had seemed like an insurmountable obstacle, but her determination and daring had enabled her to mount this barrier successfully. The blue bicycle, with its quaint frame and worn saddle, would always remind her that when you know what you want, all you need is the nerve to take it. Now she could relax in the knowledge that when the final bill came, she had the money ready.

When she returned from her adventure, the money had all been spent. She had a couple of hours before Peter would arrive home from the airport. Before she unpacked her bags, she made a cup of coffee and sat by the phone. Finally finding time to listen to the many messages that Peter had left for her while he had been away, she felt relaxed and comfortable. The exuberance in Peter's greeting made her realise that the first message was no ordinary one. He could hardly contain himself as he told her about his sudden financial success. Some time ago, he'd made a small investment in some shares, on Damien's advice. At the time she'd thought it a terrible waste of money. Peter was now telling her that the little investment had made them a lot of money. They had been sold for no less than four thousand pounds! In the messages that followed he talked about what they could do with their windfall. Another message was to warn her not to worry if he was home later than arranged. As Damien had acted as his stock broker, he would call in at his apartment on the way from the airport and collect their profits. The final message came like a bolt from the blue. Peter reassured her that he would be back on time after all. His words seemed to spew out from the machine, as he went on to say that Damien had informed him that the money was already in Jenny's hands. Peter was upset that she hadn't called him to let him know. She could feel her heart pounding as he told her that he was sure she would have banked the money immediately. His voice softened as he told her that worries about the phone bill were not necessary now they had some money behind them.

She was panic stricken. What would Peter say when he realised that not only had Damien given her the money, but she had spent it, all of it? How could Damien have done this to her? Why hadn't she stayed away from the Blue Bicycle? Peter didn't know about the huge bill she had incurred during his absence and, though it was now settled, there was no money left. The shock that she felt on realising what had happened that fateful evening was overwhelming. How could she tell Peter that the money was all gone? Then she remembered the sexy stilettos she'd recently bought. Worn with the right accessories, they may help to get Peter in the right frame of mind before she told him the news.

When she heard him turn the key in the door, she was in the

bedroom. He called out her name and she answered, asking him to wait in the hallway so she could model her latest purchase. Once again she struggled to descend the stairs elegantly in her high heels, but as that was all she was wearing, it didn't really matter. Peter's eyes were transfixed. He had seen her naked body hundreds of times before, but it had never looked quite like this. The full, round curves of her body seemed to shout at him and he suddenly became energised as she reminded him that he could touch her breasts as well as look at them. They didn't manage to make it upstairs before he fully responded to her invitation. Her adventure at the Purey Cust Bust Clinic had been worth every penny.

Afterwards, Peter climbed the stairs, exhausted. Just as he was about to sleep, she whispered to him. "I've spent the four thousand." He opened his eyes and looked at her naked body. "I can see you have," he mumbled, and smiled as he kissed her. Rather than being concerned, Peter was thrilled. He couldn't hide his delight at the results of her spending spree. They would manage without the money; some things were worth economising for. She knew that he would have as much pleasure from her purchases as she would.

As he slept, she emptied her drawer of the selection of Wonder Bras she'd collected over the years. She wouldn't need them anymore. Admiring her voluptuous reflection in the mirror, she marvelled at her new curvaceous body. "Breast enhancement is an amazing thing," she whispered, as her hands traced the outline of her body. She squeezed her breasts and giggled with satisfaction at the shape and size that her new breast implants provided. Sliding back into bed and snuggling up to her husband, she was now the proud owner of an amazing pair of assets. Whatever Damien offered or promised her, she knew without doubt that this was one investment that he would never have shares in.

The
Mature Student's Tale

Gwyneth Highley

"Yet preye I yow that reden that I write,

Foryeve me that I do no diligence

This ilke storie subtilly to endite..."

The Second Nun's Prologue

She is spewed out of the carriage with the rest of the early morning commuters. The cold air hits her after the stifling heat of the train. Her ears are assailed by the familiar voice on the tannoy, that of the Yorkshire Asian. He has very clear diction and his hybrid accent fascinates her. She scurries with the crowd, ant-like, up the steps, over the bridge, past the newsagent's with its familiar stand of newspapers, past the fast-food shop – with the assistants stacking shelves with plastic-wrapped sandwiches and cans of synthetic-tasting drinks – and out into the bustling street. The echoing noises of the station are replaced by the sounds of rush-hour traffic.

Yanking her rucksack into a more comfortable position, she inhales the morning and changes pace as the college library doesn't open until 8.45. She feels sorry for all those briskly overtaking her with their minds focused simply on work. She enjoys this part of her day; she enjoys every part of her day. Walking past the 'homeless' person sitting at the edge of the pavement, begging, she remembers how up until recently she had felt sorry for the people she had seen in this situation; but that was before she had witnessed the 'watch' being changed with naval-like precision and become aware of the sleek business which appeared to be behind these particular street beggars. She overtakes the queue of cars lined up, waiting for the command to 'go,' their occupants isolated and cocooned from the joys of this beautiful city. Pausing on Lendal Bridge she watches the ducks in their Red Arrows formation. There is a lone woman skuller who resembles a water-boatman. The pleasure boats are not yet out and the river is twinkling and peaceful in the early morning sun.

Having left behind the coats of arms and the white roses of Yorkshire which decorate the bridge, she takes a left-hand turn and strolls through the Museum Gardens, away from the sounds of traffic and into a brief time of calm and tranquillity. Wet grass means that she keeps to the path which winds around the park, past brooding pigeons and under the overhanging trees with their disappearing squirrels. Soon the last of the wallflowers will be pulled up, but for the time being she is still able to enjoy the faint smell being teased out as the sun begins to heat the air. A ring of tiny brown toadstools is just visible under an ancient horse-chestnut tree. "A fairy ring," her mum used to say. If you didn't believe in fairies you would never see them. She believed in them as a child but, to her intense disappointment, never saw one. Part of her still held a small hope that there might be such things; delicate, ethereal creatures who flitted about doing good.

As she continues along the path under the dark-green yew trees, she hears snuffling sounds and just catches a glimpse of a hedgehog vanishing into the thicket of shrubs. She passes by the wall that had been part of St. Mary's Hospital and takes in the elegance of The King's Manor where a notice informs her that the refectory is open to the public. She promises herself that she will have a coffee there, soon, so that she can see inside.

She emerges from the park and progresses past the art gallery, where the decayed statue of William Etty looks sadly down at the fountain. He seems to agree with her that the shallow rectangle, with its blue, peeling base and tired jets of criss-crossing water, is disappointing. She pushes the button at the lights on the corner and, while she waits, gazes up at the rooflines of the wind-tunnel which is Gillygate.

St. John's College is an old building, with beautifully kept grounds behind a hedge-fronted Lord Mayor's Walk. She used to see it from the car and always wondered what it would be like to be able to walk into such a building. Now she is part of it. She enters the library, which is a maze of corridors lined from floor to ceiling with books. Underneath the threadbare carpet the floorboards groan their familiar grumbles as she makes her way to the innermost part. She selects a niche overlooking the front entrance to the college and glances out of the ivy-framed casement. A gardener is busy tidying a border and an ambulance rushes its way up Union Terrace towards the hospital.

She carefully puts her pad of file paper onto the old wooden desk, surrounds herself with books and begins to work. She loves working in the library, which wraps itself around her. She feels comfortable. The books have become familiar friends. She knows exactly which bay and which shelf she needs to go to. Hours of browsing, tasting, gorging on the stocks of knowledge stacked upon the shelves, were moving her steadily towards her goal; filling the compartments in her mind left empty while she looked after her husband and daughter.

Her husband is at home, probably sitting in front of the TV. He even eats his meals in front of the television, while she and her daughter sit at the dining table. The previous night she had served him a homemade hot pot. She'd salted and peppered it and had taken it through to him, where he sat waiting with a newspaper spread on his lap. He'd been grateful and had smiled his thanks. She'd known that the baked bean stains on his shirt from earlier were soon going to be added to, but she hadn't let it bother her. She loves him.

In her second year she is taught by a new lecturer. He is stocky, but neat, with twinkling blue eyes. He gives the impression of being tall because he is confident and so enthusiastic about his subject. As he sits discussing Goethe, she admires his clean checked shirt, which he wears tucked into stone coloured jeans. He explains to the group about the Enlightenment, simplifying complex ideas. He has an innate understanding of the difficulties that the students are having and goes out of his way to explain the intricacies of science and reason. All the students are grateful for his easy approach to the subject and his desire that they should share his love for the period. They ask questions which they would hesitate to ask anyone else, for fear that they might look silly. His resonant voice pleases her as she absorbs the new material. Who would have thought that she would be sitting here discussing eighteenth century German literature? They have a coffee break and she chats to him about an essay she's writing on Swift. He reminds her about the importance of the body in 'Gulliver's Travels' and recommends a book. He munches on cheese sandwiches, which have been made with white bread. She's surprised, as she thought that an academic would be automatically more health conscious and therefore a brown bread man.

On her way back to the station she stops off at a now familiar haunt to buy tickets for Ibsen's 'Ghosts'. Standing on the highly-polished wooden floor, she hears the clatter of china from the café and a delicious aroma encourages her to think that she'll make garlic bread to go with the lasagne she's planned for tea. Handing over her student credit card, she recalls the intimate space of the Studio Theatre where women picked their way through the debris of the Trojan Wars. Swirling smoke from smouldering remains choked, smothered. A helpless baby was horrifyingly put to the sword. Against such heavy odds the women couldn't hold out and fell to the conquering army. Euripides' speeches moved her to tears, as she joined these women in their brave, but futile, struggle. Tickets pressed into her hand transport her back from Troy to York.

York Railway Station has become an old friend to her. She sits on the cold seat, watching a woman handing mints to her friends with the air of a priest handing out communion wafers. A man, wearing spats and a brown suit, spills his coffee in his hurry to catch the London train. She joins the other passengers looking skyward, scanning the neon boards. To her surprise she is joined by the lecturer. Away from college he is able to be even more relaxed and they chat freely. There is a mutual attraction. A shock-wave passes through her body as his arm accidentally brushes against hers. She notices his watch nestling in the manly hairs of his suntanned wrist. He shouts above a revving locomotive engine and suggests they go for a drink.

In her third year everything changes. The library has been absorbed into the new Fountains Learning Centre. She walks into the enormous entrance area and can't believe how open and exposed everything is. The comfortable, familiar nooks and crannies have gone. She gazes up to the highest level of the three-floor building. She sits by a small table, which has a circular wooden top and a square silver lozenge for the base. The combination of shapes is pleasing. She leans back on the cuboid easy chair. The seat is spongy and her weight sinks into it, but the back is a short subtraction sign and she can't get comfortable. She shifts her position and sits sideways. Her eye is caught by the silver cylinder-leg of the chair. It has a little fold at the end, like the lip on a pottery vase. The carpet is wall-to-wall blue with little dots, which look random, but after close examination she finds that they make up a complex repeating pattern. Gunmetal rectangles with corrugated insides are radiators, which break the continuity of the grey metal and glass panels that constitute the outer walls. She gets up and deposits her pineapple juice carton in one of the silver, bullet shaped bins. An English student in a library full of mathematical signs – incongruous.

Black rainy night. Amber street-lights glow like long Modigliani faces under round metal hats. She sits in the reception area of the Learning Centre, waiting to exchange some notes on T.S. Eliot with a friend. Silhouettes of frail, newly-planted trees sway from time to time as a bus or lorry passes. The lights of the library are reflected in the black window. The square mosaics of the air conditioning units in the ceiling are hanging from nothing outside. Her headache throbs. Is she a housewife, mother or student? She is tired, fed-up. She wants to be at home.

She is so tired that he offers to wash-up. He washes up with manly precision, but in her yellow rubber gloves. The routine is highly organised. Everything is stacked up on the side. He fills the bowl with piping hot water and a huge squirt of washing-up liquid, so that the result is a look-alike cappuccino. His idea of washing-up is to push down on the brush as firmly as possible, so that all the bristles are splayed and then to scrub it round and round until it is impossible for the bristles to return to their original position. When this has been achieved he thinks that the pot is clean and miraculously it is. A new washing-up brush will have to be bought tomorrow, but it's worth it to have one chore less to do.

She begins to sew the craft badge onto her daughter's Brownie waistcoat and is watched closely by a pair of huge cow-eyes, which scrutinise the positioning, monitoring the precision of the task. Each stitch is an effort, but each stitch is one step nearer completion. She thankfully cuts the thread and allows her eyelids to close for one glorious minute, only to be jerked back into the here-and-now by a high-pitched voice demanding her attention. A pile of ironing hidden behind an easy chair is a rising high-tide, threatening to wash over the living room floor. Making a huge effort to concentrate, she talks her daughter through the list of spellings set for the weekly trial tomorrow morning. It's already late, so a hot-chocolate and a slice of 'Harry Potter' helps the younger version of herself prepare for bed. If only a magic wand, or one of Professor Snape's potions, could ensure that tonight will not be a round of drinks of water and trips to the loo.

After tiptoeing downstairs and gulping down two painkillers with a glass of icy cold water, she can begin work – college work. Two hours of study are essential if she's going to meet her essay deadline. Sitting at the large pine table she is aware of the regular rhythmic tick of the clock. The gentle hum emanating from the refrigerator in the adjoining kitchen almost lulls her to sleep. She forces her eyes to take in the title of her latest essay about post-Modernism taking 'a stance of irreverent pastiche concerning cultural tradition' and notices that she also has to discuss the 'playful and schizoid' aspects of the genre. She picks up her copy of 'The Passion of New Eve', now transformed into a fluorescent frill of post-it-notes. Her microscopic examination of the text continues. The chair creaks as she shifts her position.

Under the debris, the table is marked with the scars of the ages; scratches resulting from an over-ambitious jump by the family's fat feline; a biroed word from a small child who'd wanted a more permanent memorial than scrap paper. A green hole-punch is just visible beneath a pastel-patterned ring binder bulging with work. A pair of worn oven-gloves is still on the table from teatime. There is a single pink sock lying behind some textbooks and a blue moisturiser tub lies on a forgotten PTA notice of forthcoming events. Her pen dents her forefinger as she struggles to write. Dull sounds of voices can be heard from the late night TV programme in the other room. There is an unmistakable crackle of a sweet wrapper being undone. Her mind has become a sludge of ideas and images, sliding around like fried eggs, which slip away at every gentle prod of the fish slice. She needs to take some notes from Jamieson's 'The Cultural Logic of Late Capitalism', but decides that the college photocopier will have to do the job for her in the morning. Tiredness can no longer be fought. She robotically goes through her bedtime routine and sinks thankfully into a cosy, hot-water-bottle warmed, bed.

As she walks towards the Minster, the autumn breeze flaps at her black gown. She takes the mortar board off her head and tucks it under her arm. Crowds of similarly clad victors are gathering together with their proud supporters. The atmosphere is joyous and those not wearing black gowns are dressed as wedding guests. She perches on the wall under the still green canopy of leaves. Birds are twittering above her. Across the road, a ladder scrapes on the hotel wall as a window cleaner adjusts his position; it must be difficult with the flower-filled window boxes to negotiate. She notices that the bright pinks and rich, green foliage enhance the building, but they have recently been watered and the window cleaner is getting wet. St. Michael-Le-Belfry nestles in the shelter of the Minster, like a small child holding the hand of a towering protective parent.

She watches as a disappointed group of tourists turn away from the explanatory sign: 'Minster Closed for Graduation'. Mums with pushchairs roll by her. There are women, with the spoils of shopping trips in carrier bags, making their way to the bus stops. A group of Japanese tourists excitedly brush past her, chattering in their native tongue, cameras round their necks and bum-bags slung round their waists. She thinks to herself that the men always seem to have cropped hair and smartly pressed clothes and they always look intelligent. Cars turn round in the circle in front of her, their fumes mingling with the smell of perfume left in the wake of a passer-by. Some drop off parties for the Minster, while others have simply lost their way and are trying to get back into the main stream of traffic. On the other side of the street, she watches the miniature train with its black and gold livery as it continues its cycle of setting down and picking up passengers for the National Railway Museum. Excited children clamber into the small carriages, followed by their more self-conscious parents. Two tattoo-covered youths, surprised at the sound of the train's hooter, stop for a moment to watch as it slowly chugs away.

The Minster clock booms out the half hour, momentarily drowning all other sound. She will soon be making her way inside. There's a shout of greeting. Her husband strides across the road, hair cut short and wearing a smart grey suit. He has been off to park the car. His smile tells her just how proud he is of her achievement. She is proud to have him here to share her special day. As they hold hands to walk over to the Minster, the breeze flips his tie up, revealing a faint sauce stain on the white shirt below.

Leonard's Tale

Matt Charnock

"Ye lye heere ful of anger and of ire,

With which the devel set youre herte afyre..."

The Summoner's Tale

I awoke with the gentle sting of the too familiar kiss of Rose, whose lips had awoken me every morning. Only today's sting was sour, the morning had not quite taken its vengeance on my eyes, or on my conscious, yet I knew she was leaving. For good. I watched, through squinted eyes, unknown to her, as she dressed and let herself out of the bedroom and into the kitchen. I listened as the familiar roar and calm of the kettle played a tune in my head. I had the time, I could have stopped her, or at least make her know I knew. But instead I lay, lying, and lying, I still lay.

A while after she left the house, I found my feet and enjoyed the cool floor and pad and fall of naked sole. The kitchen offered me a haven of familiarity. The kettle was furious with me, spitting water in my face, trying to blind me like a spoilt child not grateful for the day you have just spent with it. I made myself my morning coffee and sat in the living room, my settee groaning in a way it only does in the morning, as if it too has been awoken – possibly by the kettle's tantrum. I flick between channels – morning TV sucks. Either old news presenters talking calmly and softly as if to subdue you into what's happening in the world, telling us in a manner we usually reserve for an elderly relative: that an earthquake has destroyed an entire country, and follow it rather neatly with an article about pet grooming for the weak-bladdered. Or, and only slightly more preferable, is the young upstart jumping about telling us how excited he is for the weekend and making some off remark about the guests, followed by more about how great he is. Morning TV is somewhere between cocaine and valium. I skip breakfast, as I usually do, mainly because I cannot be bothered eating in the AM.

Rather reluctantly I get dressed. Today I am single again, and to be honest I don't care, I never cared for her, it was just fucking – but she brought emotions into it and so it ceased to be 'just fucking'. It happened when one night she brought me a gift – it was a shirt and with that she screwed the whole relationship. Anyway, I am up and I have to go to work.

I own a nightclub on Micklegate, quite a lucrative nightclub, actually. Micklegate is perfect for drinking, a circus of idiots. It took a while to think what to call it, I wanted something moderno cool (whatever), but most of the names would be wasted on my clientele, for example, a French-themed bar called Bar Dow, deliberately spelt wrong – as who would want to come to the bar dot? Bar Humbug was scrapped, as who wants to laugh at Dickensian references while swigging down ale? And there were more; Bar Celona (Spanish theme), Bar Ohmmeter, Bar Gain (offering discount beer), Bar Bar Black sheep, Bar Bar Bar Bar Bar Baran and so it went on. In the end I opted for Bar 28 (which annoyed the people at Bar 38, next to the City Screen in the town centre). Anyway, whatever it is called, it is not without irony that I own a place where people come, because I hate people. They're dumb, panicky, unpredictable, noisy, inconsiderate and they get me angry.

I have severe anger management issues. People often claim to have a short fuse and, well, I have no fuse. I can erupt over the most trivial matter. It is unpredictable. Someone could spit in my face and I might not react, and then someone might ask me for spare change only to find their head being used to panel-beat a car. I have had to go to court. Some tourist once asked me for directions to the Moat House Hotel, and after a mouthful of abuse I dragged him there by his hair and smashed his head on the service bell. He spent a week in hospital. Anyway, it seems I was 'temporarily insane' according to the jury – they gave me community service and I had to see a doctor for anger management sessions.

It is interesting to be described as 'temporarily insane', as it means you are not bonkers, but have moments where you are. Where is the line? Some Greek philosopher did a thing with acorns, where he kept putting one acorn down at a time and asking a volunteer if that was a pile. After a while, let's say eighteen, the volunteer would say that it was indeed a pile; the point was that seventeen acorns did not make a pile but eighteen does, so what is the difference between insanity and temporary insanity? One acorn. Or something like that.

Normally when I feel this rage coming on, I have to stand in a place on my own and do some Yoga breathing that was ·taught to me during one of my anger management classes. I think this is why Rose left me; I never hit her, but when I lose it I turn into a tornado. I've wrecked our – my – house many times and I think maybe I had done it once too often. The last time was the time my rages became a heap, my last acorn, and that was that. Maybe it wasn't, maybe she was bored, or didn't like the way I buttered my toast. There are so many reasons people want to leave people – whatever it was, she is gone and my life can carry on as I am sure it would have done, even if she had not left.

I opened the club as usual at eight, and as usual no one came until nine. I often thought about opening at seven to see if anyone would come at eight, but could never be bothered and so never did. I rarely go down into the club by choice. I realise that part of my job description is to schmooze people, and so I accept it; today I plan on going down at about midnight. In the meantime I intend to sit in my office, enjoy a Jack and coke with one lump of ice and watch some TV. By this I mean I am going to watch the security monitors. I never watch them for trouble, but a voyeuristic pleasure, of all these people believing that they have to do something with their lives and the thing they choose tonight is to spend the money that they earned during the week on my club. Each one having spent hours getting ready, just to look like every one else. The indie kids, trying desperately to look different, inadvertently create their own style of similarity. Dance chicks daring each other to wear a shorter skirt than the last, and then hiding the legs that they are showing with ridiculous fluffy boots. There are others as well; we get Goths coming in, with their unkept hair and combats on and ripped shirts and spangley stuff, looking like some army that taste forgot. It amazes me that they all come to my club, these different creatures with their different hunting grounds and mating rituals, but here they all are, all looking for the same thing. Quite what, I don't know; but they all seem to want it and I seem to offer it.

It is always when I am doing something else. This time I was sitting in my office, not doing anything, which became the thing that I was doing, when my walkie-talkie hissed and cackled at me in attempt to destroy the pleasure I was getting from merely sitting. Some drunken joker was claiming that he was on the guest list; my bouncers were saying he wasn't, or something like that. To be honest, all these people are the same; they are just trying to get something from me. They get a couple of drinks in them and they think that they are entitled to anything. The only thing you are entitled to do in my club is spend money – money that I will keep. Anyone doing anything other than that will be thrown out. When you own your own club, you can run it how you like. I always wanted to say something like that to them, but I usually end up smacking them round the head with whatever is at hand. Something was bound to happen sooner or later; we had started having trouble a few weeks ago. The average life expectancy of a club is six months; this is month four and therefore not likely to last much longer. We're over the hill and the club has the scars to prove it.

I left my office and started to make my way to the door, brushing the usual faceless friends off my shoulders as I walked past – girls draping themselves on me wanting to be the next ex, but living the high life on my account until that time came. I hate those bitches. No hope, no skill, just a pair of tits and blow-job lips. The usual excited 'hi's' from those who were excitedly high. Needless to say, my blood was beginning to boil. As another drunken stinking yob latched on to me and offered to buy me a drink, I snapped. I jabbed him in the throat with some move I had no idea I could do, and I saw the trouble at the door. My teeth locked together as the anger rose, every sinew in my body contracted. I stalked toward him gathering momentum, everything around him was black, tunnel vision, I had my mark. Instinctively my hand reached out as I passed the counter and grabbed the unclean, green glass ashtray, two steps later I was behind my bouncers; the man was shouting something at them and they were holding him back. I swung the ashtray and landed the blow full in his face, splintering his nose. That shut him up. I swung again; this time I landed the blow on the back of his head and sent him into my two bouncers, spilling blood on their clichéd white shirt and bow ties. They seemed unfazed by this, too used to it, too afraid to argue. They brushed him off and he hit the deck.

I dropped the ashtray on his chest and walked back into the club, nobody touched me this time; nobody wanted to buy me a drink, apart from one tosser who received a cracked shin for his offer. I sought solitude in the toilet. I locked myself into the middle cubicle. I could feel the power surge, my hands automatically went into fists, my spine needed to buckle, my whole body contracted, and then it happened. A pulse. The power, the energy from my body dispersed, sending ripples of energy through the cubicles, forcing doors off hinges, destroying toilets. At the end I felt marvellously calm. I could breathe again.

Looking around the toilet I couldn't believe what I saw, shards of cheap MDF walls littered the floor, water gushed from every possible pipe. 'Close the club,' I whispered into my walkie-talkie to anyone that was listening.

There is a strange serenity that descends when you are in a club on your own. Almost like it is the end of the world and you are the only one left alive. I pace around and look at the damage that was inflicted tonight. Broken glass here, ripped chairs there, spillage, the forgotten purses and jackets, a demolished toilet. I go behind the bar and help myself to a drink; I stare at the room that was the toilets. Taking a sip of my Jack and coke (one lump of ice) I can see something on my hand. I take a closer look and reveal that my skin is burned. Not black and crispy like a piece of meat, but slightly charred; more alarmingly, there appear to be bubbles of flesh where the heat has started to cook my skin. I tear back my shirtsleeve and the bubbles go all up my arm. Slightly alarmed, I rip my shirt open and, sure enough, the bubbles of flesh and burned skin are there as well. I look into the mirror that hangs in the bar, and see that my face bears the same scars. When was I near a fire? At what point tonight did I even risk setting myself alight? I look like I have just walked through a barbeque.

Suddenly I find that I am running back to my office, where I charge the TV up and seize the security video from the machine. Maybe someone from the club did this. I watch with intensity my movements across the club and into the fight outside. Girls draping over me, nothing wrong, people buying me a drink, seems fine, smacking the guy in the throat, no – wait. I pause the video and look at my outstretched hand; there is what looks like smoke coming from my skin, and the forming of a bubble. I fast-forward to where I am outside with the ashtray, and there, I see the full horror of what happened, of what I did to that guy. Moreover, I see my face on the screen; I see the blistered skin forming and I see the smoke, but I see no fire, no cause. I think back to the toilets and the fact that they had exploded when I was in there. I ran back to the toilets and stood in the cubicle, or rather where the cubicle was, and sure enough there was a scorched pattern where I had been. What the fuck?

I was near the Knavesmire, sitting in Dr. Barrov's office studying the mounted display of disease and trophy pictures of charcoal-coloured hearts warning of smoking. The trouble is, it looks so bad it looks fake, and therefore we can distance ourselves from it. We compare it to something from a film and we allow ourselves to become detached, in order to for us to be guilt-free when we get cancer and sue the tobacco industry – which is like cutting your arm off and suing the company that made the blade. I smoke, and have chosen to smoke and take all that comes with it.

Dr Barrov has asked me to write in order to help me 'quench my rage'. "Why don't you read it out loud?" he suggested

"Why don't you?" I said in feigned anger.

"I need to hear your speech. If I read it, it is just words; if you read it, it has emotion and that is what we are dealing with," he cooed.

"Fuck off." I snorted.

"Of course, if you don't want to, I am sure we can find a cell for you to stew in."

A pause.

I want to punch the room, I want to break it, I want my hand to bleed. I need to know the pain and I want the room to feel it and to demonstrate it. I want the visual evidence of other destruction than the destruction I have in myself. I want to punch the room.

I want them to shut up – in fact I need them to shut up – I don't want to hear the droning, nagging voices discussing their problems and manifested fears of failing themselves by doing nothing. Shut the fuck up. I want no more of their rancid tongues, licking and eating my head.

For God's sake, how much more do I actually have to listen

to? The room is shouting, cheering, egging me on – it is asking me to hit, to strike; it forces me to think and take note of all the breakable, wooden, fragile tools, hearing them asking for me to destroy them – and I can. I am powerful, more powerful than you could imagine, more than I am afraid to admit.

I grab their heads and smash them into the table to make them stop and make them stop and make them realise what they are doing and what they are saying and make the room stop.

I can't cope any more with the tedious temptations of magnolia and can't feel an end coming. I want to rip the walls out and I want to tear them down – I want to devour them, I want them to be the testimony of what I have become and what I feel, and I want the talkers to walk through the room, through the devastation that is left in my wake, I want them to walk in silence, and only when they have left may they talk again.

At the end I feel exhausted, my mouth dry and tongue clicking on the sandstone that has become my teeth. I feel too that something has been ripped out of my chest and, blackened with the tar from my cigarettes, is being waved in my face to mock me. I feel like I have just had an unwanted rectal exam and the need to vomit is great.

"Interesting," nodded Dr. Barrov. My shaking hand reached for the room temperature water, which did nothing to quench the thirst that had thrust itself upon me and forced my throat to close. My breath slowed until I no longer realised I was breathing. But I felt calm.

"I want you to continue writing."

"Whatever," I coughed, what the fuck was this? I came to talk about my anger, not my creative side. I could see where this was going, I was going to end up having poetry nights in my club, bespectacled, skinny students with long hair and smoking roll-ups, talking about the nonsense that they think they feel. I did poetry at school and thought it was shit.

The taxi pulled up and I climbed in, I barked to the driver where I wanted to go. And then I felt it start. York traffic was, once again, at a standstill. Before I knew what was happening, my hands were into fists and I could feel the blood surging, and screaming through my body, the hand that was on the door handle seemed to spasm and ripped the handle off. I caught the driver's eye in the rear view mirror, I could see the look of contempt he was giving me. He started yelling in some broken English language and that was it, I felt the pulse. It erupted from my body, blowing the passenger doors clean off their hinges, the windows splintered, the roof shredded. I stepped from the wreckage of the car and strolled to where the quivering wreck of my driver lay. Smoke seemed to be leaping from my body with pride. The car lay in ruins behind me. But I was calm again.

I had decided to walk the rest of the way. I couldn't see any driver letting me into a car when I looked like I had just been flame-grilled. After a moment's contemplation, I had decided to cut my losses and not reopen the bar. To be honest, the thought of closing had been on my mind for some time. I wanted out and this seemed like the perfect opportunity.

The bank gives me the statement of my account and I walk onto Parliament Street feeling unusually happy, despite the fact that I now have no future and no job. I have just made a substantial amount of cash from the sale of the premises, plus what I had made from working. I'm unemployed, but with means, and that makes all the difference. I stare at the fountain for a minute and realise I need to get some kind of order in my life, and I need a coffee. All this night work has not made me the best during the day. I see one of those branded coffee houses that are everywhere in York, looking slightly empty, and walk in. This is the first time I have ever been in one of these places and, to be honest, it will probably be my last. Why the fuck is there so much coffee on offer? What happened to the days when if you ordered a coffee it came from a percolator that had been on all day? Why the hell do I want half milk in my coffee? If I wanted that much milk I would have asked for a glass of milk. What the fuck is a mocha latte? And an iced mocha latte? Why would you want to have cold coffee? I order a normal, run of the mill, bog-standard coffee.

"Would you like milk?" inquires the server, whose name is Jan.

"Err...yeah," I reply to the somewhat obviousness of her question.

"Hot or cold?"

"What?"

"Would you like the milk hot or cold?" She seems a little frustrated now, and to be honest, it is not the trickiest question to answer.

"Why would I want hot milk? That's what you want to drink when you cannot sleep. If I have that in my coffee it will cancel the caffeine, and where's the fun in that?" I say.

"Cold then."

"Thanks." Whatever happened to service with a smile? My coffee tastes of mud and, because I have a wooden spoon to stir it with, I have splinters floating in my coffee like sharks – each one waiting to strike my jugular. The rim of the mug is too thick and every time I drink I feel little waterfalls of coffee flowing off my chin. The handle is too small – how does a person with hands the size of mine manage to hold what is surely a child's cup handle? All in all, I am getting pissed off.

I leave my coffee and head onto Coney Street. Not to go anywhere, but just to enjoy the very freedom that I have acquired. It is when I get about ten paces into the street that I realise that schools are on holiday and everyone has decided to come to York for the day. Why the fuck would you want to come to York? There is nothing here. A wall maybe, but look at your house; there is a wall there too. People not knowing which way they want to go, or what attraction to see, instantly make my temperature rise. Is it that hard to pick a course and stick to it? In fact, if we were all to do just that, we would all get to places much quicker. What is worse are the people who suddenly stop, like that fucking robot in the Wizard of fucking Oz, or whatever. This makes me have to turn to avoid them, thus crashing into someone else, which annoys them and I get the blame. I start to walk harder, tightening my shoulders and I do not flinch or move from people's paths. If they stop, I crash into them and that is their fault, despite the fact that they also blame me. Maybe they are right, maybe it is not everyone else who should pick a course and stick to it, but I who should walk around the town like a dyspraxic butterfly. I try to contain it, I try to breathe like Dr. Barrov had said. I don't react, but I can begin to feel the skin on my back blistering. An old lady pushing a pram spies me and I can nearly hear her shout 'Ramming speed', as she bashes that baby bus into my legs.

"Watch where you are going."

"Sorry, I didn't see..."

"No, you didn't see because you can't fucking see, you stupid old witch," I storm off, "for fucks sake."

This shouting seems to be working, it seems to release some of the pressure, but I can feel heat rising and smoke coming from my collar. After a bit more abuse the police arrived.

"Don't touch me!"

"I think you had better calm down."

"Don't fucking touch me!"

"I need you to calm down so we can put you in the van peacefully; we can't have you terrorising people."

"Don't touch me. I don't know what will happen."

"All right, tell us what you are on, so we can help."

"I am not on anything, I can't fucking control it."

"Control what?"

"I'm about to fucking explode, I can feel it."

"OK, where are the explosives?"

"There are none, it's me. *I* am about to explode." A small crowd started to gather during the conversation I was having. Two more coppers had arrived and they were making some sort of fence with their bodies. Most people just walked past and pretended not to notice what was happening, but then the fucking tourists started to watch like it was some piece of street theatre and that gave the Brits the permission they needed to watch as well. I saw one of the coppers talking to his radio, asking for more help and the bomb squad, and this just angered me more. I leapt towards him, grabbing the radio. I ripped it from his uniform and smashed it into his face. He reached for his baton as he hit the deck, but I stamped on his hand and shattered his wrist bone. The other coppers made their way over as I seized the first guy's baton and cracked the head of the nearest person. I cracked him again, spinning. Another copper sprayed mace in my eyes; I screamed in anger and pain. My hands now blistered and smoked. Two coppers saw this and backed off. The skin on my head was popping with heat and smoke. I clench my fists, my head goes back and I feel the rage rise like magna from a volcano.

Credits to GMTV finish and the lights come up to reveal a man and a woman on a sofa.

Man: Good morning. We begin today with the tragic and strange news of an explosion in York yesterday.

Woman:	A man was so angered by the number of tourists that he took frightening action – setting off explosives that brought the city centre to a standstill.
Man:	Fortunately no one was injured in the blast, which ripped through many shops in the vicinity and destroyed several vehicles. The police are stunned by the lack of physical evidence, and have been unable to find a trace of the explosive device used.
Woman:	Eyewitnesses say that the man appeared to set fire to himself moments before the bomb went off. So intense was the blast, that pathologists were unable to identify the body. A team of experts had to reconstruct data from a surveillance camera in order to identify the man.
Man:	One expert believes, however, that the suspect in question was not a terrorist, but a victim of modern life and living. Joining us in the studio is Dr. Barrov. Now, Doctor, you were the individual's physician, correct?
Dr. Barrov:	Yes, that's true. Leonard was a patient of mine and I don't believe that he was a terrorist. In fact, I believe that due to the anxieties and pressure he was feeling, he quite literally exploded.
Woman:	Surely, though, there would be some physical evidence of this?

Dr. Barrov: Actually, it is the very lack of physical evidence that has led me to this conclusion. The police cannot find a device, or indeed any sign of explosives; in fact, all they have is eyewitness testimony that states a man 'Blew up'.

Man: Astounding, whatever next?

Woman: Now, have you ever had trouble in keeping your garden looking great?

The G.P.'s Tale

Maggie Cobbett

"The sely housbonde, algate he moot paye..."

The Shipman's Tale

Nobody in the village knew how old Old Yorkie was. Nobody except myself, of course, and he'd already been long retired when I inherited his medical records. From the tall tales he told the regulars in the Tiger, he could have been born at any time during the last century – although only the highly gullible or those in their cups really believed his reminiscences about trench foot, shell shock and the effects of mustard gas. His eyes used to twinkle with mirth and good humour, especially at the offer of a free pint of Sam Smith's, and when he chortled they disappeared altogether into the deep wrinkles. He loved to tell newcomers that his nickname had nothing to do with either football or chocolate, although he *did* support York City, of course. Rowntree's was an easy cycle ride from his parents' house in Marygate, but Yorkie had never wanted to work anywhere but on the railway, like the rest of the men in his family. This ambition had been fostered by many happy memories of trips to the seaside, made possible by his father's travel concessions. The young Yorkie used to dream that one day the tracks would extend under the crashing, grey-green North Sea as well, so that he could explore the lands on the other side.

He got his chance, although not in the way he'd imagined, when his call-up papers arrived. His new mate, Scouse, re-christened him when they met as raw recruits and struggled to understand each other's accents. They survived Dunkirk, managed to stick together throughout the North Africa campaign and kept each other's spirits up during the long crossing to Normandy. Seasick and hungry at the same time, they plunged from the landing craft into the cold and choppy water of the English Channel. For Scouse, the Longest Day turned out to be his shortest, but Yorkie made it to Bayeux, picked up the piece of shrapnel from which he nearly died and spent several months in hospital before he got his discharge. As a small tribute to his mate, he kept his nickname for the rest of his life.

He liked to talk about his late wife, although there were few people around who remembered her. He used to bring out a battered photograph of a pretty, but rather stern-looking, dark-haired girl in a floral dress and recall how they met one sunny afternoon on the neat gravel path of the Museum Gardens whilst he was convalescing. Her brother, an airman home on leave, recognized Yorkie from a fight they'd once had at school over a gobstopper. He introduced his sister and they all ended up eating together at Betty's Bar. Romance flourished over the spam fritters and Kunzle cakes. Sadly, it was to be Mrs Yorkie's last meal with her brother, but I think you might still find his name at Betty's, scratched onto part of the old mirror downstairs in the Oak Room, along with the names of other young airmen, including many Americans.

Before the war, Mrs Yorkie had been in service at the old Haxby Hall, close to her parents' home, and had had an excellent training in plain cooking. She was a godsend to the NAAFI canteen at Fulford Barracks and, when it was all over, to the shy man in the demob suit who led her proudly down the long nave of St. Mary's. After a few more years on the railway, he tried to persuade his wife to consider a holiday abroad. It was a big source of regret to him that his only real opportunity to travel had been in wartime, when everything he'd have liked to see had been bombed out or boarded up. Unfortunately for him, Mrs Yorkie was of a more practical turn of mind and insisted that most of their savings should go towards buying their own home. She did allow Yorkie to run an old Austin Seven though. Lovingly polished every weekend, it took them to visit Mrs Yorkie's sister in Nether Poppleton and her cousin in Tadcaster. Once, they even ventured as far as Fountains Abbey, but Mrs Yorkie was adamant that, even before it was ruined, it wouldn't have been a patch on the Minster.

Little Crossing was their pride and joy. The long garden at

the back of the cottage allowed Yorkie to grow all the vegetables and fruit they needed and to keep a few hens. He sang out cheerfully whenever his wife brought him down a cup of tea and it was always the same song, *My gal's a Yorkshire gal*. Their little front garden was a riot of colour. No one in Haxby or Wigginton combined could compete with Yorkie when it came to sweet peas and he managed to have something in flower almost all year round. Mrs Yorkie was a model housewife. She cooked, cleaned and polished all day long and stuck to the routines drilled into her as a girl. After a certain date each year, no matter what the outside temperature, the cosy fire in the sitting room disappeared and was replaced by a dried flower arrangement. Yorkie never grumbled about taking off his boots on the back doorstep, having his fingermarks removed from the furniture and his feet from the shiny brass fender, or climbing in between icy cotton sheets in their unheated bedroom. As long as he had Mrs Yorkie to keep him warm, he was a happy man.

They never had any children, but just accepted, as people did in those days, that it was not meant to be and doted on their nephew, and godson, Stephen instead. The boy was always sure of a warm welcome and a good meal from the simmering stew pot on the black-leaded range, or a piece of the latest Victoria sponge cooling on the scoured wooden table.

After Mrs Yorkie died, the winter after their Silver Wedding, Yorkie continued to work in his garden, did his best to keep the house as she would have wished to see it and retreated to the Tiger whenever he felt the need for company, which was often. Nobody could remember when Yorkie became Old Yorkie, but I think that grieving for his wife etched more lines into his already weather-beaten face and bowed his broad shoulders.

Apart from Stephen, the person who paid the keenest attention to Old Yorkie's tales was Desmond Bilborough. Many years before I took over the local practice, he and his wife, Edna, had moved in next door to the Yorkies and, at Edna's insistence, modernised their cottage to within an inch of its life. It wasn't long before she developed a burning ambition to buy out the Yorkies and knock through into their cottage. Mrs Yorkie wouldn't entertain the idea, no matter how much Desmond was able to offer. Edna's disappointment was so acute that she accused her husband of meanness. One row led to another and in time she left him, the word *miser* ringing in his ears. Desmond was distraught and convinced himself, even after their divorce, that she would return to him if he could only get his hands on the Yorkies' cottage and create her dream home. It became an obsession with him, but he had to wait until Mrs Yorkie became ill and he had his neighbour at his most vulnerable.

Their savings were small, but Yorkie wanted the best for his beloved wife; a fire burning constantly in the shell shaped grate of the little cast-iron fireplace in their bedroom, a private hospital room when he was no longer able to cope and finally, a send-off to be proud of. None of the family could understand why Desmond Bilborough spent so much time with Yorkie during those dark days. Neighbourliness was one thing, but the man was never off the doorstep. At the funeral tea, he was positively proprietorial, handing round the ham and tongue sandwiches and tea in the best Crown Derby cups. It was the first time anyone had seen them outside the big mahogany china cabinet, and he had even been into a sideboard drawer for a crocheted doily to put under the fruit cake.

'Acting as if he owns the place,' sniffed Yorkie's sister-in-law. Of course, as they were soon to discover, he did. In return for enough money to ensure Mrs Yorkie's comfort and dignity in her last few months and a small allowance for its maintenance, Yorkie had signed over all rights to the cottage after his own death. Stephen, who by that time had broken with family tradition and joined the Merchant Navy, had insisted that the agreement should include provision for the possibility that Desmond might die first. Both men had laughed heartily, thinking of the decades between them, but shook hands on it. Yorkie assured his neighbour that, if his war wound didn't carry him off, it wouldn't be long before his dicky ticker did.

The only thing that bothered Yorkie was that he wouldn't be able to leave the cottage to his nephew, as he and his wife had always intended, but Stephen was not one for cupboard love. He told the old man not to give it another thought and continued faithfully to send him a postcard from every port of call. Yorkie studied them avidly, stuck them into an album and got out his old school atlas so that he could follow Stephen's voyages around the world.

As the years went by, Yorkie hardly seemed to change, but Desmond Bilborough grew older, greyer and increasingly frustrated. Even when Edna married Mr Poyse, senior partner of the firm of estate agents Poyse, Cann and Ukit, he couldn't let go of his dream and monitored every cough and wheeze he heard over the garden fence. Several times he had the gall to quiz me about Yorkie's famous shrapnel wound and general state of health, as though he'd never heard of doctor-patient confidentiality. The day Yorkie fell off his ladder whilst trying to prune one of his fruit trees and was rushed into hospital, the paperboy swore he heard a champagne cork popping next door. It was a black day for Desmond when his neighbour emerged from the ambulance and, cheerful and sprightly on the crutches he'd been taught to use by the friendly physiotherapists at York Hospital, made his way up the path to his front door. Bilborough's face was as white as the plaster cast on the old man's leg and that night he had a massive heart attack. As no relatives could be traced in time and his ex-wife wanted nothing to do with it, Yorkie arranged his funeral and raised several glasses to him in the Tiger afterwards.

The day after Bilborough's funeral, Yorkie sent for Mr Poyse to do a valuation. The amount quoted made him blink. He agreed to sell immediately and telephoned Stephen, who'd retired from the Navy by then. They put their heads together, bought a big motor home and headed straight for the North Sea ferry terminal in Hull. They've been travelling around Europe for a couple of years now. I got a postcard from Yorkie only last week, telling me that they'd made it as far as Istanbul and were just about to cross over into Asia. His wife may never forgive him for selling Little Crossing, but Yorkie will certainly have plenty to tell her when they meet again.

The Student's Tale

Imogen Featherstone

"Herde I a millere bettre yset a-werk.

He hadde a jape of malice in the derk."

The Cook's Prologue

It was Toby's round. He lurched from the bar to the table where his new housemates were sitting and plonked down their drinks. A pint of bitter for himself, lager for Richard and a cider for Ginnie. He had been feeling a bit shy earlier, but four pints on he felt more at home, blearily confident.

"So this'll be your local too now, mate," commented Richard. "You'll probably find you'll be spending a lot of time in this place from now on."

Toby looked around to take in The Green Dragon: heavy flock wallpaper, old guy propping up the bar, York Brewery beers on tap. Lovely.

"This'll do me just fine," he said, turning back to them. He caught himself looking at Ginnie a moment too long. Her creamy skin. Shining black hair. That little turquoise t-shirt showing off her bellybutton and her heavy breasts. He'd have to watch it. Moving in with a couple could be a minefield.

Not too sure about Richard either, he thought. It was the dodgy T-shirt that did it. A picture of a house with the legend *Hot Property* emblazoned above it.

"So, what happened to your last housemate?" Toby asked.

Ginnie and Richard looked at each other. Richard leant back slowly and slid his arm around Ginnie's shoulder before answering.

"Jake? Well, it's a complicated story." Richard ran his hand through his hair, then stroked it into glutinous peaks. "We didn't really know him before. I mean, I know we haven't known you very long, but this was different. We thought he was a bit of an odd one even before he moved in. We'd met him in the union a few times in the first year, always on his own. Wearing brown cords and a peaked cap that made him look like an extra from 'Oliver'. He was very keen to get to know us, just not that good at it. He'd strike up a conversation, then grin awkwardly until a pause became an embarrassing silence. Then he'd sort of writhe and shuffle off."

"We thought he was probably just shy, you know," said Ginnie. "I felt sorry for him. So when he asked us if he could stay with us for the summer, we said yes."

"We needed the rent," added Richard. "If we'd known how it was going to turn out, we'd never have agreed."

"How do you mean?" asked Toby. The turn the conversation was taking was rather worrying, but he was intrigued.

"He was a tosser," said Richard. "Sounds awful, I know, but if you knew how he was to Ginnie, you'd agree."

"Yeah. Good job I had you to sort him out," said Ginnie, smiling and leaning her head against Richard's shoulder. "We weren't going out then," she explained.

"And Jake thought he was in with a chance," said Richard. "As if…"

"I remember when he arrived at our house to move in," continued Ginnie. "I was the only one in. I answered the door and there he was: all gangly legs and lank hair. He was lugging two great big bags with clothes spilling out of the top. A dirty-white shirt with flouncy collars and cuffs, and stained red knee-britches. I asked him what they were.

"'Oh,' he said, 'I'm working at York Chamber of Horrors for the summer. It's my costume. I'm Mad Jack. I shout at people in the dungeon all day.' You could tell from the way he said it he was really proud of working there. Like it made him really interesting.

"I remember standing in the kitchen with him a few minutes later, waiting for the kettle to boil. He stood with his legs wrapped around each other, looking at the floor and surruptitiously scratching the eczma on his elbows, while I tried not to watch him doing it. He flushed when I spoke to him and as soon as the tea was ready he scuttled off to his room to unpack. At the time I just thought he must be feeling shy, first day in a new house and all that, but now I wonder if he'd already got a crush on me."

"I reckon," said Richard. "I remember how he used to look at you."

Toby looked up sharply. Had Richard caught him looking at Ginnie? But Richard continued to speak to Ginnie, oblivious, "And, although he was always the odd one out, he did relax a bit with me and the lads. But he'd go quiet when you were about. Or do something stupid to try to impress you."

"He did really out-there things to impress us all," explained Richard to Toby, "But the focus was always on Ginnie. It was like when you're at junior school and there's a kid who fancies a girl in his class. But instead of talking to her nicely, he jumps on her back or pulls her hair or something, do you know what I mean? Except that it went a bit further than hair-pulling."

He squeezed Ginnie's hand.

"I have to say though," he continued, laughing, "It was funny the first time he brought a little surprise home from work."

"I guess so," said Ginnie, breaking into a smile. "You all certainly thought so."

"We were in here one night," Richard explained, "With Jake and a couple of mates from my course. Jake was more chatty than usual. He loved telling us 'wacky' anecdotes about work. He was telling us about Old Nell, the wise-woman, who had an unnaturally close relationship with Eli, the plague victim dummy. He'd always start off, 'Something dead funny about the Chambers is...' Then he'd tell you some limp story and throw in a couple of puns for good measure. But I was glad he seemed to be relaxing with us, anyway."

"I liked some of his stories," said Ginnie "About going into town as Mad Jack at lunchtime and..."

"Yeah, right," interrupted Richard, "Very funny. But we're getting off the point here, aren't we? Where was I? That night, when it was Jake's round, he came over from the bar, dished out the drinks and we all carried on. Then Ginnie lifts her glass to her mouth and all of us, simultaneously, notice. All eyes fix on her glass. She looks down. There's an eyeball looking back up at her. Yellow and veiny.

"'Uh!' she goes and jerks her glass up. Half her cider leaps out and lands in her lap. The rest of us are pissing ourselves laughing, we just couldn't stop. Jake was really pleased with himself. I remember slapping him on the back and saying, 'Good one, mate.' Of course, I checked out if Ginnie was alright too. But you took it in good humour, didn't you? Fished out the eyeball and chucked it at him, if I remember rightly. It was a good night. We just didn't know what was coming, did we?"

Ginnie took up the story, "I started to think he was seriously weird when we went along to The Chambers of Horror. Have you been?" she asked Toby. Toby opened his mouth to speak. He had been and he'd loved it; the 'blood and guts' humour and the way it got you thinking about our history. But Ginnie wasn't actually interested in his opinion. She continued to give her own, without giving him a chance to speak,

"Well, I wouldn't recommend it. It's very seedy. Jake was the worst, in his torture chamber. Although I have to admit he looked the part, gaunt and sallow. I don't know if he was always that bad, or if he exaggerated his performance for our benefit. He was screaming and moaning. Bullying the punters as he showed off his torture instruments: the Rack, the Boot, the Gibbet cage. Threatening to boil them, roast or behead them. Some of the parents looked rather alarmed. Then he accosted an American couple and screeched into their faces, 'Well, of course, you'd know all about methods of torture, wouldn't you?' I mean, they were on holiday for God's sake.

"We waited for Jake behind the scenes afterwards, so he could come to the pub with us when he'd finished his shift. We sat in the kitchen chatting to Tina, aka Old Nell. She had changed out of her costume because she was about to pick-up her kids from school. She still looked like Old Nell, though: moon face, gappy teeth, bulbous eyes. But she was lovely. And she agreed that Jake was O.T.T. She said she thought it was only a matter of time before he got the sack, the way he was carrying on. Of course, I didn't tell Jake what I thought. Just said I'd had a good time and thanks for the tickets. You and I had a good old chat about it afterwards, didn't we Richard?"

"Yeah, we certainly did," replied Richard. "You really weren't impressed were you? I have to admit I really enjoyed the whole blood-curdling experience. I thought it was great fun. Although Jake did act like a twat. I certainly don't blame you for telling him what you thought, after what happened next."

"It was a couple of days later," explained Ginnie, "I was working in a shop for the summer and had to leave the house at 8.30. I'm not a morning person. I trailed downstairs in my dressing gown as usual, still groggy. Put the kettle on. Groped for the cornflake packet. Tipped it up. 'Thunk'. There's a rat in my cornflakes!

"I jumped back, hyperventilating. Its beady eye was looking up at me. It didn't move. It was dead. When I'd caught my breath, I moved closer to it. It had cornflakes sticking to its fur. I poked it with my spoon and it rolled over, stiff. I didn't know what to do with it. I needed to go to work and I couldn't just leave it on the kitchen counter. But it made me shudder to think of touching it. I decided to go and get Richard. I knew you'd sort it out for me. When I turned around, Jake was poking his head around the door, grinning. 'Aha, you found it then,' he said. Realization dawned. It was one of his bloody jokes. He darted into the room, dodged past me and grabbed the rat. He swung it by its tail in front of my face, leering and laughing. 'Say hello to Ginnie, Mister Rat.'

"I was livid. I yelled at him, 'Look, Jake. Just get that disgusting creature away from me.'

'You don't have to worry,' Jake taunted, 'It's not going to bite. It's stuffed. It's one of the plague rats from work.'

"I shrieked, 'Just sod off. I don't know what you're trying to achieve, but I've had enough of your pranks, alright?'

"He stopped waving the rat at this point.

"I continued, 'I'm sure you think it's all just harmless fun but you're doing my head in. I just want to be able to relax in my own house. Without having to worry about rats in my cornflakes or creepy crawlies in my tea or whatever else you've got up your sleeve, alright?'

"Jake was wincing, but that only encouraged me. Now that I'd started to put the knife in, I had to drive it home. I screamed, 'I think you're pathetic. Repulsive.'

"Jake laid the rat on the kitchen counter. He sat down on the sofa and looked out of the window. He was silent.

"I was a bit shaken by the force of my outburst, but I grabbed my bag and left.

"At the bus stop I bumped into Tina, aka Old Nell, taking her kids to school. I told her, in a furious torrent, all about Jake's rat 'joke' and the row we'd just had. She was totally on my side. Turned out he'd been bragging about his antics at work. She thought he was an idiot. Anyway, her kids started making fart noises and collapsing into giggles. Then the bus came and we sat together and talked about TV. I offered to babysit, I could do with the extra cash, and gave her my number. By the time I got off the bus, I'd forgotten all about Jake and his rat."

"Jake certainly didn't forget about it though," commented Richard. "When I came downstairs he was crumpled on the sofa. He looked like someone had knifed him. He looked up at me, red-eyed, and pushed past me, up to his bedroom.

"I left him to it. But when Ginnie got home I asked her what was up with him. She told me about the rat and how much it had upset her and my hackles went up. It wasn't on. I gave her a cuddle and told her I'd sort it. I banged on his door and had it out with him."

"I remember, I could hear you from downstairs," said Ginnie, grinning. "You yelling 'What the hell d'you think you're doing, picking on Ginnie?' And him whining back, 'It was only meant to be a joke. You thought the eyeball was funny. You're just siding with Ginnie because you fancy her.' I have to admit I liked hearing that last part. Then he sidled past and legged it downstairs and out of the front door.

"He lurked around for the next few days, simmering and resentful. When me or Richard came into a room he'd leave, slamming the door behind him. He rushed up to his room after work and ate his meals up there. After several hostile days, I decided to make the peace. It wasn't that I wanted to take back anything I'd said. But I was sorry I'd shouted at him. So, on the bus home from work I rehearsed what I was going to say. I got home, kicked off my shoes and trudged upstairs to take off my uniform. I opened my bedroom door and my stomach plunged. I shut the door and backed across the landing, gulping for air like a goldfish. I ran downstairs, headlong into Richard who was halfway up. He asked me what was wrong and I gasped out, 'my room.' He told me to wait downstairs."

"So, what was up there?" asked Toby.

Richard continued, "Well, I legged it upstairs, adrenalin pumping. I don't mind admitting I was scared of what I might find. I flung open the door. It was dark in there and as my eyes adjusted, I breathed in a sharp, acrid tang. Urine. I peered into the dim light and that's when I saw it: A man hung from the clothes rail, his head flopping forward onto his chest.

"'Oh my God.' I winced and looked away. Then forced myself to flick on the light and look again.

"It was a dummy. Fake blood on its sacking costume. Fake eyes rolling. My heart was still banging away in my chest as I yanked it off the rail and hauled it downstairs. I showed it to

Ginnie. Jake had gone too far this time. He'd even pissed on the floor. I was going to punch him out. I barged upstairs and into his room. Empty. He'd cleared out.

"Ginnie was relieved. 'Saves us the job of chucking him out,' she said. But I was all hyped up. I wanted to hit him. And I knew where to find him.

"Ginnie told me to cool it and calm down. 'I know you want to get him for me,' she said, 'But let's be clever about it. Let's play him at his own game.'"

Ginnie took over the story, "Over the next few days we planned together. Sat up late into the night, sharing a duvet on the sofa. Getting closer. It was exciting."

Toby's flushing face told Ginnie that she was embarrassing him. She warmed to her story, "It was electric. That's when we got it together." She leant over and pressed up against Richard. She kissed him, her eyes watching for Toby's reaction. Toby looked away, uncomfortable. "And what was the plan?" he asked, not at all sure that he wanted to know.

"Well, I phoned Tina and asked her to do us a favour. I explained what Jake had done and that we were planning to play a little trick of our own, although I didn't say exactly what. On the day that we'd chosen, Tina left work early to pick up the kids as usual. Only, before she left, she pinched Jake's keys from his jacket."

"Let me tell it," said Richard, jigging up and down on his chair. "Let me tell it how it must have been for Jake."

"Okay," agreed Ginnie, "You'll tell it better."

"Just imagine," smirked Richard, "That night Jake is the last to leave the building. He reaches the door and finds that his keys are missing and the door is already locked. 'Damn,' he grunts, and heads back towards the cloakroom to see if his keys have fallen out somewhere. As he hurries along the corridor, the lights go out. It's pitch black. 'Shit,' he thinks, 'A fuse must have blown.' He clicks on his lighter. The flickering light illuminates blood-stained walls. Glassy-eyed dummies lurch in and out of his vision, as he makes his way carefully through the gloom. A darting movement at the edge of his sight makes him turn. Nothing there. Just deep shadow. He is jumpy. 'Calm down,' he says aloud to himself, 'Deep breaths. There's nothing to worry about.' His voice sounds odd, disembodied in the darkness. He carries on along the corridor. A few moments later, he hears a light, skittering sound, like rats running about in the ceiling. The sound grows louder, rhythmic, thudding. He turns and runs back along the corridor. The banging follows him, pounding above his head. He runs into his dungeon and slams the door. The air is filled with blood-curdling screams and metallic clanging, like dustbin lids crashing together. The lights go on.

"A dummy hangs from the ceiling, wearing brown cords and a peaked cap. A carving knife sticks out of its chest. There is a folded piece of paper attached to the handle. Jake takes a deep breath and steps towards the dummy to have a closer look. Daubed on the outside of the paper are the words, 'Mad Jack' smeared as if with bloody fingers. The dummy is suspended high, so that Jake must reach up and pull out the knife to read the message within the paper. He steels himself, reaches up and yanks out the knife. Slippery entrails splatter out of the knife hole, landing on his shoulders and upturned face, a bloody mess. He wipes his eyes, spits and unfolds the piece of paper. He reads 'Mad Jack: Don't Come Back.'"

Richard leant back, hands behind his head, legs outstretched, satisfied.

"That's the last we saw of Jake," said Ginnie, smiling. "He didn't come back to uni after the summer. Good riddance to bad rubbish, I say."

Richard leaned towards her and they kissed, long and hard.

As Toby watched them he felt panic rising in his chest. 'Who the hell are these people?' he thought. 'Drunken student pranks are one thing: shaving off your mate's eyebrows or writing 'wanker' on his forehead. But mock suicides and murdered dummies? That's just sinister.'

Toby stood and walked out of the pub. He would find somewhere else to live.

A Child's Tale

Anthony Webster

"I wol yow telle a myrie tale in prose..."

The Parson's Prologue

"**W**hy on earth have you bought *six* of those? They weren't even on the list." The question was as inevitable as the response each time dad did the supermarket shop.

"They were on special offer – two for the price of one. You can't miss an opportunity like that." The rest of the conversation would similarly follow agreed lines, like the steps of a well-rehearsed dance.

Ever since his redundancy, dad had insisted on 'doing his bit' for the household. It wasn't that he was completely out of work, but his hours were now more part-time and spasmodic, giving him time in town to do the basic shopping – and at times pick me up from school. I was, however, surprised when, the next day, I got a message during last lesson that he was waiting for me in reception. I knew something was wrong.

"Is it mum?" I asked, anxiously as he stood to greet me. He was trying to look relaxed, but the tension in his face was clear for all to see.

"No, love, it's not mum," he replied, "It's Meg."

Meg was our Border Collie – but more than just a dog to me and my parents. She was the revered elderly resident of our home; at seventeen years old, my senior by several years. It shouldn't have been a surprise; she'd been unwell for some time and was clearly getting worse in recent weeks. But it was a shock.

"Is she…?" I couldn't say the word, but dad understood.

"Mum's sent for the vet to come out and see her." The tears welling in his eyes were the clearest answer – she would be by the time we arrived home, and I hadn't even found a minute to fuss her that morning before rushing off to school. We sat in silence all the way home. The skies outside the car reflected the sombreness inside.

It wasn't actually as bad as I expected when I saw her, and I realised then why I'd been picked up so promptly. There she was, lying on the settee as she had done for much of the time in recent weeks, still on her blanket. The vet had only just left. She was still warm – and still Meg. I cried, of course I did. But stroking her and saying goodbye still seemed natural. She wasn't cold and she wasn't stiff. I could see that, as dad carried her out. Dad put her at the bottom of the garden under the azalea bush. It was raining hard by now and he looked a pathetic sight, but I think he preferred it that way.

It wasn't long afterwards that mum brought up the subject at dinner.

"It's time we thought about getting a new dog, you know."

My heartbeat increased and I looked at dad. He'd stopped in mid-chew, his eyes filled with moisture again. I thought at first he wasn't going to reply. But he did – eventually – he didn't look at either of us.

"We'll never replace Meg," he said simply.

"I'm not talking about replacing, love. I'm talking about getting another dog. I don't feel right here alone all day on my own."

"But you're not on your own. I'm here more now."

"No, you're not. Not really. You just don't have work to do all evening when you finally get home. You're still out more days than you're in."

"But what about the cost? I'm not earning regularly now."

This verbal tennis match went on throughout the meal. I don't know why dad bothers – he always gives in to mum in the end. Eventually the white flag went up.

"Oh do what you like. But don't expect me to…"

Mum just smiled. Dad always said that when he threw in the towel – and he always eventually did what he said he would refuse to do at the outset. Like the hanging baskets which he wouldn't water, or the village magazine he wouldn't help her edit, or the cat litter he wouldn't empty.

It was two days before she made her next move, again at the dinner table.

"I wrote to Mr James today," she announced.

"Who?"

"Mr James, you know, the farmer."

I was as baffled as dad. There were plenty of farmers in and around our little village of Rufforth then, all well known to us, but no Jameses.

"Which farmer?"

"The farmer we got Meg from."

"What for? To tell him she's…died?" He still didn't like to say it.

"Well, I mentioned that, of course, but I was really writing about our new dog."

Dad just looked puzzled, a fork-full of potato halfway to his mouth, so mum continued.

"I wrote to ask him if he was still having puppies on the farm, and if he might have one that could be related to Meg, and…"

Here dad broke in.

"That was seventeen years ago, love. What chance is there that his dogs now are from the same line? Come to think of it, what are the chances that Mr James is still alive, let alone farming? He was our parents' age, remember? It'd be a darned sight easier to go to the RSPCA; at least you'd be doing some poor dog a favour."

Mr James's reply came within the week. Yes, he thought he could remember the young couple with the two children, and he was so pleased that Meg had proved so special to us and, as it happened, he did have a bitch, Jess, we could have, if we wanted. She wasn't a pup; she was thirteen months old and was proving to be a poor working dog. He felt sure she would make a good pet and yes, she must be related to Meg, because all his dogs were just pups from his earlier bitches who'd 'caught on'.

We set off quite early on Saturday; the sun was breaking through the clouds and blue patches were beginning to appear as we entered the city. Everywhere I looked, I saw dogs. Acomb Green was alive with them on their early morning outings: big ones and small ones; shaggy ones and smooth ones. We travelled through York and back out into the openness of the countryside beyond the Hopgrove. It was about seventy miles to the farm, but the nature of the roads meant a good two hours in the car. Next to me on the rear seat of our estate car lay Meg's collar and lead; I fingered them often on the journey. The mixed emotions of sadness for the past, and excitement for the future, sent strange electrical pulses through my body.

The farm was picture postcard, set by a stream just off the minor road on the edge of a hamlet, all mellow stone buildings and roses rambling over the front door. Mr and Mrs James couldn't have been more pleasant – storybook grandparents.

"I'd stand back if I were you," said Mr James, with a chuckle in his voice as he reached for the latch. I thought I was prepared, but the released energy of the bundle of white fur which shot from the barn, took me completely by surprise.

"Down, Jess, down," shouted Mr James, and eventually the excitement subsided sufficiently for her to realise that she was being spoken to and she did settle – well at least to some extent. Enough at least for me to realise that she was black and white, like Meg. But there was so much white on her that even with the dirt of the barn, the overall effect was that of freshly fallen snow. Her coat was more like an Old English Sheepdog's in length than our Meg's.

"I'm afraid this is her problem," continued Mr James. "She rushes around everywhere in excitement and doesn't listen to a word I say. It's not that she's deaf – she can hear her food being prepared from the other side of the yard. It's just that she can't concentrate."

"Sounds like someone in my class," I thought, but said nothing. She was, Mrs James explained, probably worse today than normal, as they had decided to keep her in the barn until we arrived. She had spent quite a lot of time in the barn or the yard in recent times as Mr James's son, who now did most of the work on the farm, had found life in the fields easier without her than with her. This would have automatically endeared her to dad. It was what he thought about himself when he was made redundant. "My absence is more valuable than my presence," he would mutter when mum tried to encourage him.

"What do you think, then?" It was dad trying to be practical. He knew perfectly well what we thought – and what he thought. We'd all fallen in love at first sight with this amazing ball of energy – and she clearly loved us with an even greater intensity. But once dad gets into one of his practical moods, he sticks with it, so having settled the first part we moved on to the second.

"We haven't even discussed how much you want for Jess." He addressed Mr James with a business-like tone in his voice that suggested that he could well change his mind if he couldn't drive a decent bargain.

"Oh, we don't want any money for her," retorted Mrs James, "Do we Jim?"

"Never even considered it," he said. "Just pleased if we can find her a good home."

"Really!?" Dad could scarcely conceal his delight. "You don't get offers like that everyday."

"No, dear," interrupted mum, "Another offer you can't resist, if you ask me."

The following week had a stop/go feel to it. Whenever I was at home, the time simply flew, but school dragged. All three of us walked her every day. I'm sure she was getting more exercise than she had had down on the farm, yet she was putting on weight – quite noticeably. We decided it was the shower and shampoo we'd given her. It fluffed up that great mass of mainly white fur, so much longer and denser than Meg's, into a huge cotton wool ball. But then mum noticed she was having more difficulty getting through the dog flap in the back door. I was quizzed about chocolate drops I may have given her, but pleaded innocence. Dad said we should cut down on her food and only give her dry food rather than the cans she preferred – and definitely no leftovers.

The weekend was busy. Dad was travelling north to spend some time with my gran. She was due into hospital for an operation on her eye and he wanted to be there when she came out, so he'd refused any work for that week. He left on Sunday morning. The fuss mum made, you'd have thought it was my brother or sister going off to university for the first time.

"Have you got your drink? Promise you'll stop every two hours at least. Remember to phone as soon as you get there – and each time you take a break. And don't forget to give our love to mum – and buy some flowers for when she comes out." Eventually he left.

Mum's friend, Sofia, arrived at about 3.00 in the afternoon. I like Sofia, she's different. She used to live on a boat. A bit younger than mum and dad, but you can tell just by looking at her that she never quite left the seventies, never stopped being a hippie. She looks after all the pampered pooches for miles around and drives everywhere in her little white microvan with hand-decorated side panels: 'Grooming Marvellous'.

She'd come to see Jess. "What a lovely dog. There's nothing more handsome than a long-haired Border Collie. And so much white – quite outstanding," as she petted our adored and adorable Jess, who rolled over, as usual. "You do know she's pregnant?"

Mum went white.

"She can't be," she stuttered eventually. "The farmer would have told us. They know about these things. I think we've just been over-feeding her."

She was grasping at straws now, but Sofia just felt Jess' tummy gently with both hands.

"No question," she affirmed, "and look at her teats."

"How long?"

Sofia squeezed a nipple and, to my amazement, I watched a thin cloudy liquid issue forth.

"Tomorrow, a couple of days maybe, can't be definite."

Mum had sat down at the dining room table. She was mouthing words, but nothing was quite getting out. Mum, so organized, so reliable, always knowing what should be done next, didn't know what to do or say. I did.

"What will we need to do, Sofia?" I urged.

"Hopefully very little – the most important thing is to find a good place out of the way, make her comfortable and let her get on with it. Let's see where we can find."

We left mum at the kitchen table sipping hot, sweet tea with a glazed look on her face as we started our rounds. We quickly rejected the greenhouse (too hot in the day, too cold at night), the garage (too many dangers for the pups, and the cats had permanent access) and the cubby hole under the oil tank (too small). I was beginning to despair when Sofia asked if she could use the loo. Since we were just outside the back door, I directed her to the one downstairs. She'd not been in there above ten seconds when the shout went up.

"Perfect! We've got it – the perfect spot."

We made a barrier across the room with two bales of straw from Sofia's van and scattered some straw from a third over a piece of plywood. Sofia explained that, in the first few days,

Jess would be able to come in and out as she wished, but the pups would not be able to get over the straw barrier. Apparently, so Sofia said, mother dogs can find their pups irritating at times and it's good if they can get away from them for a while.

By the time we'd completed our task, mum had recovered herself and Sofia had to leave for a shampoo and cut for a dog in the next village, but I was in charge now and it was just as well, as mum needed me.

"What will I tell your dad when he rings?" she wondered.

"Nothing, not at the moment," I replied. "Sofia said Jess might lose them. She's only a young dog."

"But that would be awful," moaned mum.

"We'll just have to pray that it turns out all right," I said.

"Yes – no – oh, I don't know anymore. What is right?"

We put Jess to bed in the downstairs loo that night, and she seemed to like it. She slept better than we did. Me and mum met several times during the hours of darkness. She didn't even get cross with me, or query why I wasn't in bed. But nothing happened. At breakfast time I became unwell, headache and so on. I thought it better to have the day off. After all, mum needed me and I didn't want to miss something so educational by being at school, did I?

The day dragged and by 5 o'clock, I wished I had gone to school. I'd missed art and PE, and nothing had happened. It still hadn't at bedtime and we were both facing another sleepless night. Fortunately mum was back to her old self and dealt perfectly with dad when he rang. He, of course, was more interested in updating us on gran, completely unaware that another drama was unfolding at home.

It was 11.35 pm on my bedside alarm when mum woke me. I'd have sworn on oath that I hadn't slept, but I must have done.

"Ssh! Put your dressing gown on and come quickly," she

whispered. When we got downstairs, the sight that met my eyes seemed as if it was coming from a film. There was our lovely, white fluffy Jess lying in the straw and already, alongside her, were one, two, three unbelievably small, snub-nosed black-and-white bundles. Mum and I didn't speak, but I could feel the electricity passing between us. We didn't need words. Before my eyes a miracle was taking place, as more wet bundles began to emerge.

"I'll pop and get the camera," she said quietly after a while. I flexed my knees to draw closer and give Jess a stroke, but she made a sudden move, as if she was uncomfortable. It made me jump.

"Ssh, steady," I whispered gently, but it happened again – and again. Her nose went towards her tail as if she were in some discomfort. Then I realised what it was – number seven had decided to arrive. So long after the others – an afterthought – or a surprise, as dad called me, born so many years after my siblings. But it was so tiny. I thought the others were small, and so they were – but not as small as this one.

"This one's mine," I said to myself. "She's like a little petal."

"I think the first one has just been named." Mum's voice came from behind me. I hadn't heard her return. "We'll have to find something suitable for the others tomorrow."

We continued to wait, but when nothing else had happened after an hour, mum persuaded me out of the loo and back upstairs.

The next day was near perfect. The sun shone, there was a light breeze – and no school. I couldn't believe my luck; the teachers had two training days just when I needed them most. Jess was happy to share her new brood with us, and mum and I made the most of it. We pulled out some of dad's decorative fencing wire from around the garden and made an impromptu enclosure on the back lawn with two huge cardboard boxes as sun shelters.

I was surprised by how much pleasure I got from just watching the pups. Initially all I wanted to do was touch them, but mum put a limit on that. I quickly learnt that observation had its own delights. They slept a lot, of course, but even in sleep they were beginning to show their individuality. And so the names came – Cuddles and Bouncer, Fluff and Jet, Comic and Dozy – and of course, Petal.

But how were we going to deal with dad? When we heard his car, we both went out of the house to greet him as he reversed into the drive. It was quickly clear that her approach was going to be the full frontal attack.

"Mmm," as she gave him a big hug, was immediately followed by, "Have we got a surprise for you! Close your eyes and hold my hand. Promise not to peep."

Dad's excitement was palpable. I'm sure he thought that somehow mum had managed to get one of those television make-over programmes in to revamp a room, or his beloved garden. He followed her trustingly, like a young boy on his birthday treat ready for his big surprise. In those few seconds I caught the first glimpse of them as teenagers together – but I was nervous that it was going to be the calm before the storm – or the volcanic eruption.

By the time they reached the lawn, dad's gait showed that he was decidedly disorientated by his temporary blindness but still, apparently, completely trusting in his partner of so many years, as his eyes remained tightly shut. By the time they reached the lawn, all the pups were snuggled together asleep in the shade of one of the boxes. Jess greeted dad enthusiastically and he responded with encouraging words and strokes of his spare hand – but still unseeing.

"Hello girl, have you and mum got a surprise for me? What is it then, hey girl?"

"When I count three you can open your eyes – one...two...three..."

"What the...? Where on earth...? How...?" was about as far as he got.

Mum's response was perfect.

"Special offer, darling. Eight for the price of one. You can't miss an opportunity like that."

Author's note:

This story is based on a real-life incident. Names have been changed to protect the privacy of the dogs.

The Tale of Griselda and the Chair

James Walker

"This storie is seyd, nat for that wyves sholde

Folwen Grisilde as in humylitee,

For it were inportable, though they wolde;

But for that every wight, in his degree,

Sholde be constant in adversitee..."

The Clerk's Tale

I would like to explain to you why I am in a room with my best friend, who is cellophaned naked to a chair. But before I can, I need to take the tights out of his mouth, and ask him myself, as not even *I* am sure how this happened. It would seem I have got myself into an awkward predicament and I haven't even been drinking.

By the way, my friend is called Walter and he is the husband of Griselda. Walter and Griselda have been going out together since they were fourteen. They were the one inseparable couple that every school churns out whilst the rest of us were happy to play hop scotch or football. The only time they stopped petting was when lessons began. I sometimes think that if they had been allowed to continue they would have done better in their exams.

Their intense love annoyed me at first, as every time I asked Walter if he wanted to do something he would decline. He'd say they were studying together, or going to see a film, or they had to do some shopping for his gran. After a while I stopped asking him because I couldn't bear to be continually denied, especially given that the diversity of his reasons always gravitated back to the same word: Griselda. I accept that there may be a slight element of jealousy in my tone. I just can't accept that he wanted to spend more time with her than I did with a football.

When we left Fulford School, he went to work on Fishergate as an apprentice electrician for his father's business and she became a receptionist. Within months they had moved into a terrace in Acomb, living well off of their combined income. As I had nobody to kiss at school, I did well in my exams and so decided to stay on and do A-Levels.

I would often pop round to their house in the evenings. I didn't particularly want to see them, it just got me out of my mother's house for a while and enabled me a little privacy. When you're at the bottom of the pile you must choose between your evils, and ruining their privacy was a lot more enjoyable than ruining my mum's.

They were good to me and would let me drink their beer for free, although I always suspected Walter was a bit of an exhibitionist who took pleasure in flaunting his emotional and financial wealth. He'd say I could pay him back one day, when I got a well-paid job and the education had paid off, but he's still waiting, as am I.

Two months and three days after Griselda's nineteenth birthday, she gave birth to an 8.5 lbs. baby boy, Mac, named after the York City legend, Andy McMillan. Griselda was not happy with the name, but had eventually given in. After a thirteen-hour labour, arguing was the last thing on her mind. Besides, she confided in me that things could have been worse, as he originally wanted to name the first-born after the squad that went twenty-one games unbeaten in 1974. I put her mind at rest by explaining things could have been even worse, that he could have wanted to name the child after the current eleven who had set the record of twenty-one games without a win.

Exactly eleven months later, Griselda gave birth to another boy. She told me that Walter desperately wanted the baby to have a brother, as he had grown up a single child. Fortunately, this time the boy was not named after a footballer. He was named after the lead singer of The Smiths. But once more, after a long, drawn-out birth, arguing was the last thing on Griselda's mind. She told him no more children and, as all his heroes had been immortalized, he assured her there was no more need for kids.

Money became scarce, as did the free cans, and I found his sudden interest in my education alarming. I think he really believed that my future job would help bail him out of the current situation. I stopped going round for a while, because listening to people arguing is not as pleasurable as listening to people talk – although what they argued about did make me laugh. Griselda kept saying she wanted to go back to work and earn some money, but Walter was having none of it. He didn't want his children to grow up with strangers. In his diplomatic way, he told her that he would give up work if she could get a better paid job. It was a fair point, but something about it seemed wrong. There was no way she was going to get the same money as an electrician, not unless she got an education, and she couldn't get an education while she had to look after kids.

All of a sudden, Walter wanted to meet up regularly for a drink at The Swan, on Bishopthorpe Road; I think he had used up all his kisses and now wanted to find a different use for his mouth. He would sit and tell me how unreasonable Griselda had become and how she seemed to be more interested in the kids than him. I didn't tell him, how she had told me, he seemed to be more interested in drink.

He would complain that she didn't understand the pressure of working a six-day week. I never reasoned with him that this was because she worked a seven-day week, as he wasn't looking for rational explanations. Instead I conveyed sympathy through the universal shrug of shoulders, as he just wanted someone to talk to, and given that he was buying, it seemed a fair exchange.

Dinner times were added to our weekly drinking routine after the birth of his third. He had a big contract at King's Square and so needed the rest to get away from all those wires. He would tell me that when he closed his eyes at night, all he could see was reds and greens and blacks. I confessed that this was more colourful than my dreams, until he explained that it was the colours of earth, neutral and live wires. He confided that their daughter had not been planned, although I sensed he was more gutted that they had conceived a daughter, and he had no female idols he could name her after. But he eventually found one, naming her Lara after the Tomb Raider character, much to Griselda's annoyance.

Walter told me he enjoyed his job, but it made him tired. His greatest pleasure in life now, was falling asleep in front of the TV or in the bath whilst reading the paper. He told me he didn't even have the energy for sex anymore and that Griselda seemed less attractive with rusk stains on her blouse. I suggested that perhaps she should feed the children something different instead, but he didn't find it very funny.

The next time I saw Walter was earlier today. He called me at 1pm and asked me to meet him down the Punch Bowl, on Micklegate. I should have sensed something was up, as Griselda had called earlier and asked me to pop around at 8pm. He had a devilish grin on his face and couldn't contain his excitement. He began by explaining how relationships worked and how it's not the same when you have seen the same body for ten years and that body has had three babies. But recently something had changed. He'd been asleep on the settee and she had come up to him and started to nibble his ears, 'Just like she used to when we were at school.' I told him I thought one ear looked slightly smaller than the other, and without thinking he started laughing.

He said that the next day she had made strange food like strawberries and cream and celery doused in mayonnaise. He then went into great detail about the way she sucked on the celery and the way she dropped the strawberries whole into her mouth – as only a frustrated married man can. It was as if he was proudly promoting a car he had rescued from certain oblivion.

"By Wednesday," he explained, "she was bending over at every opportunity and had even gone commando." I suggested that perhaps she had not had time to do the washing, but he wasn't listening. He was too busy recollecting the sight in precise detail, which was perhaps unnecessary given that she was his wife and not mine. However, each time he lusted after her she rejected his advances, telling him that tomorrow was the night. He must have been excited because he didn't make me pay for the pint, even though it was clearly my round.

When he got home that night, there were no screaming kids or TV blasting out Bob the Builder. Just a little message that read, 'Come up to the bedroom'.

When Walter got into the bedroom, Griselda was flounced across the sheets, dressed in latex. Her hair was tied back tight against her head and bunched into a long, seductive mane. Walter went to speak, as Walter is apt to do, but Griselda silenced him, running her finger across his lips. She put on some music that involved sitars and African drums and began to dance for him. He seemed to enjoy it more than when he had listened to The Smiths.

After slowly undressing him, she placed him naked on a chair and bound his arms and legs to the frame, so that he couldn't move. She then took off her rubber suit and took a pair of tights out of her drawers. She caressed the tights delicately across the indents of her body and then she rolled them into a ball. Just as Walter was about to scream out in ecstasy, she ran at him and shoved the tights as far down his mouth as they would go.

"Would you like to play, little boy?"

Although Walter was gagged his genitals spoke for him; striking upwards into a solitary salute like a raised arm desperate to catch the teacher's attention.

"Good," said Griselda, and began to apply bright red lipstick to the edges of her mouth. This unfamiliar behaviour excited Walter, as she had previously adopted the motto of 'what you see is what you get'. He began to shake in anticipation, reminding Griselda of the washing machine on full load. She then took some cellophane out of a drawer and started to wrap it slowly around his body from the neck downwards, as she had done previously with cling film around his sandwiches for work.

Walter was feeling a little nervous now, finding Griselda's behaviour most out of character. For the first time in years he didn't know what was going to happen next and was beginning to find the experience annoying, rather than pleasurable. He was just about to explain this to Griselda, when he remembered that her tights were in his mouth and the only conversation he was having was with himself. He momentarily considered the possibility that she had cellophaned him so that he lost some weight, but this soon passed when she ripped holes in the cellophane to expose his most erogenous zones.

"Baby nod up and down if you are okay."

Walter nodded his head up and down.

"Recently, things have started to get a little stale in the bedroom." Walter was nodding his head before Griselda had finished.

"So I thought it was time to spice things up. Do you want me to spice things up?"

Walter nodded his head three times, just in case he had not made it perfectly clear how much he was enjoying this fresh approach.

"Would you like some oral, baby?"

Walter was now nodding his head so fast that it actually looked as if it was stationary, like the effect you get from rotating helicopter propellers.

She bent down so that her mouth was within inches of his groin, and began to talk into the surrogate microphone.

"Would you like the kind of oral every woman should give her man now and then?"

Walter nodded his head and Griselda lowered hers. He closed his eyes, realising he was a lucky man. Then he opened them to find Griselda getting dressed before closing a fully packed suitcase she had hidden under the bed.

"You are the most inconsiderate bastard I have ever known. Every single night I have to listen to your whinging. Whinging about your day at work, whining about your dinner, moaning about the state of the house and the noise the kids make. Then if I'm not listening to your whinging, I'm listening to your snoring or listening to the phone tell me that you're going to be late or back after closing.

"I've given you everything; my youth, my adolescence, my twenties. I've given up my career, my friends and hopes. What have you given me other than stretch marks and a headache? I can't talk to you anymore; it's always you, you, you. Do you ever ask me how I feel? Do you ever ask me what I want to do? Do you ever ask me if I mind staying in looking after the kids whilst you piss away the few pence we have? I reckon you would drink the River Ouse, if it was made of booze. Just to get you to listen I have to tie and gag you. It's the only way I can get a word in edgeways. That's not how it's meant to be. That's not what love is all about. That's certainly not my idea. Well, I've had enough. I'm leaving you. I'm going to live with my sister and she's gonna look after the kids whilst I start back in my old job. If you want to see them you're welcome, but you won't see me again. You were a good sort long ago, but now you're no better than the rest. Well, I'm not having it anymore. Go get yourself a slave, or someone partially deaf. Someone that will listen to all your bloody stories about cowboy electricians who 'wouldn't know the difference between a fuse box and a trip switch if it hit them in the face'."

She then kissed him on the cheek and told him I would be around at 8.00 to untie him…and so here I am.

When I entered the room to find my best friend cellophaned naked to a chair, you can appreciate my dismay. It seemed strange that we had spent an entire adolescence avoiding eye contact in urinals and dressing back to back after PE, only to have everything flaunted in one fell swoop. It was excessive behaviour and I asked him if he had been drinking. He shook his head from side to side and I sat down on the side of the bed, wondering what I was meant to do next. My education had never prepared me for situations like this. I find it hard enough trying to make decisions concerning my own life, without confusing matters by bringing naked best friends into the equation.

I decided to do what all friends do when an unfamiliar situation impinges upon their relationship; I asked him if everything was okay and if there was anything he wanted to tell me. He shook his head from side to side and then up and down, shaking the chair he was strapped to. I decided to take the garment out of his mouth and see what he had to say for himself. As always, he was less than grateful.

"Where the hell have you been?"

But he wasn't interested in an answer and so it was I who did the listening, as he delivered a ten-minute appraisal of my life – although it felt more like a criticism. He demanded to know the reason I was so late. Why I had arrived at 9.30 instead of 8.00, as I was supposed to. He then informed me that I had always been late since he had known me and it was damned irresponsible and rude. He even suggested that my poor punctuality was the reason I didn't have a girlfriend. I just shrugged my shoulders, because he may have had a point.

It seemed absurd to be lectured on moral etiquette given that he was strapped-up naked, but I figured that this irony would sink in sooner or later. Eventually his rant turned to raucous laughter and, although I couldn't decide if it was due to insanity rather than joy, it was better than having my life dissected. He began to explain everything, and slowly it all made sense. I felt a little sad in a way that his nudity was not a presentation for my benefit, but this was soon surpassed by relief.

He told me that beer was invented for times like these, and that a pint would never taste as good as it would tonight. I agreed with him wholeheartedly, but was just a little unsure if he wanted me to carry him down to the local strapped to the chair, or if he wanted me to untie him. It's hard to gauge the boundaries with exhibitionists.

Whilst in the pub I decided not to disclose that I admired his wife, as it didn't seem appropriate. Besides, it was one of those situations again where he was back in control and it was my role to obediently shrug my shoulders as he spoke. He told me how she would be back, how she didn't understand, and how hard it is being an electrician. He seemed more angered at the unnecessary waste of the cellophane and how he would much prefer to look after kids, than wires. I just smiled and listened, seeing as he was paying for the drink.

The Cook's Tale

Maxine Gordon

"He was as ful of love and paramour

As is the hyve ful of hony sweete:

Wel was the wenche with hym myghte meete."

The Cook's Tale

'Bish. Bash. Bosh.'

Helen's stomach curdled at those three words. She turned down the volume on the remote control and looked at her five-month-old son, Rory, snoozing in the baby bouncer at her feet. Instantly, she felt calm. His skin was milky white and his chubby cheeks would have made a full moon, had it not been for the dimple on his chin. With a finger she traced its curving 'W' shape.

"I've had more than two hundred women. I started when I was twelve," the man's flat York accent drew her back to the video she had been watching.

"It was my cousin's wedding and everyone was outside watching the fireworks. I sneaked into the shed with my brother's bird for a bit of bish, bash, bosh. It was crazy. We were at it and all these rockets were going off. I suppose it meant no one could hear her screams," he paused, before breaking into a leery smile, "…of pleashurrr."

"How old was she?" asked the interviewer.

"Fifteen."

"Did your brother ever find out?"

"Sure did. Both ended up with a dose. Dirty little cow."

The programme cut to the adverts, its title flooding the screen: 'Britain's Randiest Romeos'. Helen brushed aside a tear and pressed the pause button. It was time to get her husband Tom's tea on. Tonight was their first wedding anniversary and she was making boeuf bourguignonne as a treat. "Daddy'll be home soon," she sang out to Rory, still snoring softly below.

As she placed the casserole dish in the hot oven, Helen reflected on how much her life had changed in the past year.

Until Rory's birth, Helen had her own successful business. She ran a sandwich bar, Munchtime, on George Hudson Street in York, which was open from 7am–3pm on weekdays. It had a great location in what Helen dubbed 'the golden triangle of York' and drew a steady stream of locals and tourists. On the doorstep were several large offices full of railway and insurance workers. Around the corner was Micklegate, historically the Royal gateway into York, which was lined with elegant Georgian buildings, quirky shops and inviting cafés. The third side of the triangle was completed by the railway station and Lendal Bridge, which gently arced the River Ouse and led up to York Minster.

Tom wanted Helen to sell up once they were married. He was an accountant who had inherited, from an elderly aunt, a three-storey Victorian villa overlooking Acomb Green, in the suburbs of York. But Helen was determined to hang on to her independence. She had resisted Tom's pleas to move in with him before the wedding and instead lived in a tiny, one-bedroom flat off Walmgate, a rather run down area of the city centre close to York's other river, the Foss. She loved that part of York; 'the shabby-chic end of town', as she called it. But like much of the rest of York, Walmgate was undergoing what Helen termed a 'trendification'. Luxury flats, smart restaurants, expensive gift shops and even an Italian deli had appeared in the past couple of years. Helen welcomed these changes. She enjoyed browsing in the shop windows on her ten-minute walk to work, or meeting a girlfriend for a caffé latte or light supper in one of the bistros near her flat. She knew she would miss all that when she moved to Acomb.

Tom and Helen were both twenty-five and had met in Freshers' Week at York University. With his tall, athletic frame, floppy, bright-blonde hair and owlish specs, Helen had mistaken him for an American, although he had never left Acomb. At eighteen, they'd lost their virginity to each other, which made their relationship seem all the more destined.

But seven years on, and in the run-up to the wedding, Helen

found herself imagining what it might be like to sleep with someone else. Although they had never discussed it, she wondered whether Tom had similar fantasies. After all these years, their love-making held few surprises, but Helen was pragmatic. Sex was only part of the package. Tom was kind, loving, generous. Unlike Helen, he was sensible, serious, grown up. Which was why she was confident they were meant for each other.

In the shop, Helen knew many of her regulars by name and their orders by heart, so she took notice one Monday lunchtime, about eight weeks before her wedding, when a strange face arrived with an unusual request.

"Awright darlin! Cheese'n'tomato sandwich ta, but can you butter all four sides of me bread. Don't mind paying extra."

Helen's eyes narrowed as she studied her new customer. He was of medium height, well-built and had hair as black as Whitby jet, which was sculpted into those mini cones once beloved of boy bands.

"All four sides buttered?" she checked.

He nodded, flashing a grin straight from the Tom Cruise school of charm.

"Brown or white?" asked Helen.

"For the perfect bite, it must be white," he sang, finishing with a wink.

Helen smiled to herself as she made up the order.

"There you go. One extremely buttery, cheese and tomato sandwich. One-ninety. No extra charge."

The next day he came back, with the same smile and request.

"Like your butter then?" piped up Helen.

"Oh yes," he said, his azure eyes drilling into hers. "And not just spread on a sandwich."

Captured by his stare, Helen felt her cheeks redden as she handed over the order.

"See you tomorrow," he said, eyes still set on hers. Then he crossed over the road to Beer 'n' Cheer, the off-licence run by Sam Shaw, a regular of Helen's.

By the end of the week, Helen's customers had provided the low-down on her bread-and-butter man. His name was Andy Perkins. He had just started as the new manager at Sam's shop and lived in its upstairs flat. He had a reputation as a local lady-killer and had once starred in a TV documentary about one-night stands, in which he had boasted he could pull any bird, any time, anywhere. Sam told Helen he had a copy of the documentary on video somewhere, if she was interested, adding it had been passed to him by one of Andy's 'lady friends'. Then there were the personal testimonies. Several female customers from the local insurance office had confessed to Helen they had slept with Andy. What's more, she learned, women in York were queuing-up to do likewise.

"Why, is he that good?" asked Helen incredulously.

The answer was always the same: "Even better."

In any other man, it would be enough to make Helen retch. But Andy's exuberant confidence intrigued her. He had a rough sex appeal that was new to her. Soon, she found herself looking out for him at lunchtime. He always arrived at 11.45am. He told her he liked to beat the rush…and get her on her own, adding that, ordinarily, he didn't make a habit of coming early.

It was another cheesy line, but it set Helen's mind racing. What would it be like to sleep with him? Crikey, just a few weeks earlier, the thought of having sex with the local stud would have appalled her. But now, she was longing for her daily dose of flirt-and-go. She began making more effort with her appearance, washing her blonde bob every day and swapping her apron for jeans and tight T-shirts, to show off her trim figure. She felt like a teenager again. She'd even dreamt about him. The night before, while making love to Tom, she imagined Andy's swollen lips caressing her body. It fuelled her curiosity even more.

The next morning, she felt excited as 11.45am approached, day-dreaming that this time something might happen. And then it was time.

"Anything for me to munch on today, gorgeous?"

Helen's insides quivered as she met his gaze. Then, in a surge of madness, she let loose her deepest thoughts.

"How about me?" Helen's heart froze in shock at her brazenness.

"Whoa, steady on there, or I might just take you up on that," said Andy, resting an arm on the counter.

Helen felt an adrenaline surge and upped the ante. "That's the intention. It's a special offer." She reached for the counter to steady her nerves and willed herself to follow through. "One Friday night only. Your place, say nine o'clock?"

A satisfied grin spilled across Andy's face. "Well I'm supposed to open until ten, but old Sam's a soft touch, and what he doesn't know won't harm him. Let's split the difference and make it nine-thirty?"

Her mouth dry, Helen just nodded.

Andy smacked his lips together. "Now, any chance of a sarnie? I'm famished."

For Dutch courage, Helen downed half a bottle of vodka and coke in her flat, before heading for Andy's. She took her usual route to work: up into town, past the medieval splendour of the Merchant Adventurer's Hall and towards the pedestrianised shopping precinct. Crossing the river over Ouse Bridge, she felt the arrival of that familiar wave of alcohol-induced confidence. She hoped Andy would be sober. While booze might disrobe women of their sexual inhibitions, it spelt disaster for blokes. A quick grope and an even quicker quickie was not what she was after. No, she wanted the complete works. Enough to give her plenty of fireworks to sustain her sex life in marriage and provide fantasy material for a rainy day. As she knocked on his door, she told herself a girl was entitled to a last fling.

The ring of the telephone reverberated inside Helen's head like a punch bag. It felt as if Lennox Lewis was trapped in there, desperate for an escape route. Opening her eyes slowly, she was relieved to find the familiar surroundings of her bedroom. The ansaphone clicked on. It was Tom, suggesting lunch.

Tom. She turned to the picture by her bedside. It was Tom at his sexiest. In shorts, lounging on a picnic rug on the banks of the Ouse last summer. The urge to see him was overwhelming. She dashed to the phone.

"Hi, hun. It's me. Feeling a bit ropey. Had too much vody with the girls last night. Nothing a few pellets won't sort out. And some chips. Usual place, usual time?"

Lunch date sorted, Helen sank into a bath and struggled to piece together the night before. Her mind was still fuzzy, but she remembered kissing Andy, lying on his sofa...then throwing up in his bathroom. At some point, she passed out, and came to in his bed. She was shocked to find him asleep next to her, both of them naked. A wave of nausea came over her. She hadn't, had she? He wouldn't have, would he? No, it's not possible, she convinced herself. Spotting her clothes by the bedroom door, she quietly got dressed and let herself out. The cold morning air helped sober her up and by the time she had crossed back over the river to her flat, all uncertainly had gone. She hadn't betrayed Tom.

On Monday morning, Helen steeled herself as it approached lunchtime. She had decided to play it cool with Andy. Not even mention Friday night. Hopefully, he would take her cue and let things lie. He was an expert in this field, after all. As 11.45 approached, Helen's insides were in free fall. However, by noon, the place was packed and Helen was too busy to fret about Andy. After the rush, Sam Shaw popped over from Beer 'n' Cheer for a toasted teacake.

"Not seen you for a while," said Helen.

"Oh, it's all hands to the pump today. That new manager's gone AWOL. Just packed his bags and left."

Helen stuttered as the implication sunk in. "Wh..what. Andy? Left? For good?"

Sam nodded. "Only been with us a few weeks," he said with a tut. "Young folks, don't know what side their bread's buttered."

The phrase made Helen smirk, but the thought of not seeing Andy again brought relief. She was off the hook. She'd made a stupid mistake, but there had been no harm done, she told herself. Now she could focus on Tom and the wedding. He was coming round for dinner that night, to finalise the seating plan for the wedding. Helen was going to cook his favourite, Thai Green Curry. And for dessert, she'd splashed out on some sexy undies.

Tom was enjoying a beer and pondering how to avoid placing flirty Aunt Mabel next to his grumpy grandpa, when Helen's mobile rang.

"I'll get this in the kitchen while I stack the dishwasher," Helen said, flicking open the handset. It was one of the latest models that received pictures too. She didn't recognise the number, but she caught her breath at the familiar voice.

"Hope I'm not interrupting any bish, bash, bosh with you and fiancé."

Helen froze. "Andy. How did you get my number?"

"I make it my business to get the numbers of women I sleep with. It's only polite, isn't it, to call?"

Helen closed the kitchen door and spoke in a low voice so as not to alert Tom. "Look, I know I made an idiot of myself, and I'm sorry if I led you on, but it's best if we forget the other night. After all, nothing really happened."

Andy snorted. "Nothing happened? Well, that's not how I remember it."

Confused, Helen struggled with her reply. "Well, I know we kissed and I...I...woke up in your bed, but I know I'd remember if we'd actually done anything..."

Andy cut in with a menacing tone. "Oh do you now? Well, maybe you need something to jog your memory."

The phone went dead. Helen stared at the handset shell-shocked. Next, the envelope icon filled the screen. It was a text picture. Helen pressed the OK button and swallowed hard to halt the horror rising within her. Frantically, she flicked through the menus to return the call.

"Oh my God, what the hell have you done?" she hissed, her voice full of alarm.

"Well I know you were pretty arseholed, but don't come over all Little Miss Innocent. You loved every minute of it. And there's plenty of evidence to prove it. My phone takes pictures as well. I just put it on the bedside cabinet and took some snaps of us at play. Oh, and did I mention that when I raided your phone for your number, I got fiancé's as well..."

"Stop it. Stop it now," Helen pleaded. She couldn't believe what she was hearing, but her eyes were telling her otherwise. "What is it you want?"

Andy gave out a low chuckle. "That's ma gal," he said, in an American twang. "You and fiancé are not short of a few quid, so for two grand, I'll keep it zipped. I'll call into the shop to collect on Friday, usual time."

Helen lost count of the number of times she'd been to the loo as she waited for Andy. Since his call, she reckoned she'd shed half a stone through worry. Luckily she had some savings in an ISA account that Tom knew nothing about. But what if Andy wanted more? What if Tom found out? She couldn't shake these thoughts from her mind.

As 11.45 approached, Helen felt her tummy tighten. By 12.30 she began to panic. Andy was never late. What was he up to? Customers soon became a distraction and in the melee she didn't notice Sam Shaw in the queue.

"Oh, what a palaver," he sighed. "Had the police round last night. Seems that 'Andy' bloke was robbing me blind. My bank account's been cleared and there's enough stock missing for one helluva party."

Helen struggled to process the news.

Sam went on. "I knew he was a womaniser, but never had him as a thief. The police arrested him this morning. Reckon he could get three years."

Helen's hand flew to her mouth to disguise her shock. She glanced at the plastic bag under the counter, packed with bank notes, then followed Sam to the door and flipped the sign to 'Closed'. Dazed, she walked through to the back of the shop and burst into tears.

The sound of baby Rory's cries brought Helen back into the present. She set the timer on the oven and put a bottle of the baby's milk in the microwave to warm through. Her eyes rested on a group of photographs stuck to the fridge, marking the best days of her life. There was one of her and Tom on their wedding day last year. Another of Tom cradling a minutes-old Rory. And her favourite: all three of them snuggled on the sofa at Christmas.

Helen realised she was pregnant on her honeymoon. She blamed wedding stress for the lateness of her period. But when she missed a second, she bought a test kit. She broke the news to Tom on the flight home from Jamaica. Never had he looked so happy. She surprised herself by how thrilled she felt. The thought of becoming a mother was terrifying, but now she was married, it felt right. They'd even thought of names. Rory for a boy. Daisy for a girl.

The microwave pinged. Helen snatched the bottle and returned to the lounge.

"Are you hungry, little man?" she asked, picking up Rory and tickling the dimple in his chin. Together, they cuddled into the comfy armchair. Rory's eyes glazed over as he guzzled on the teat. Helen pressed the 'play' button on the remote control. The words 'Britain's Randiest Romeos' filled the screen again. She'd never watched the Andy video all the way through. When she asked Sam Shaw if she could borrow it, he handed it over, no questions asked, but with the warning: "He's a very naughty boy, me love."

As Andy's face stared out from the TV, Helen braced herself for the feelings she knew would come. First shame, then regret and finally, sorrow.

"Forgive me," she whispered, softly brushing her lips against Rory's coal-black hair.

Then she lifted her eyes to meet Andy's and inhaled sharply as she prepared to take in those familiar features: his glinting eyes, that devilish smile and the soft cleft of the John Travolta dimple on his chin.

A Poor Man's Tale

Linda Murphy

"Amonges thise povre folk ther dwelte a man

Which that was holden povrest of hem alle..."

The Clerk's Tale

Bill, he of shocking-red locks and laughing, cornflower-blue eyes. A law unto himself. Far craftier than any cart filled with any type of monkey. A Yorkshire man of high principles and honour. Of a sunny disposition; a natural opportunist; an optimist at heart.

Being of an adventurous and spirited nature, and neither afraid of life nor of death, he drifted from place to place. It was when he ambled into York that something stirred within him; he felt he'd come home. For York had a sense of permanence and well-being about it. He earned a meagre living by keeping his finger on York's very lively and throbbing pulse and, with his canny knack of knowing what was needed, deftly turned his hand and his sharp wits to acquiring it.

In time he met the lovely Sara, who lived with her brutish, widowed father. Bill very quickly recognized in her York's northern-grit and inner strength, and he loved her for it. He loved how her quiet air could – and very often did when he needled her too much – turn verbal and extremely blunt. Sara wasn't one for having her head easily turned; but she saw beyond his tomfoolery, loving the man beneath for who he was: Bill, who loved for the sake of loving; who laughed for laughter's sake, asking only that you share in the fun. So full of life, yet defying that same life to harm either him or that which he cherished. And woe betide anything or anyone who might even think to...

It was with this in mind, coupled with the tale brought to him by his beloved's neighbour, Mary, of Sara receiving another drunken beating, that Bill was spurred-on into making Sara his own.

Bill's determined footsteps over the pavement, causing faces to peer around net curtains when he ran down the street, were nothing compared to his rappings upon the knocker. Disembodied heads popped around their doors, bobbing up and down at various heights. The older women, by some invisible signal, gathered into groups, heads together, quietly speculating. Every now and again nodding and looking towards the commotion. The rapping quickly turned to clenched-fisted, white-knuckled hammering upon the wood.

"Watson! I know you're in there!" shouted Bill. A breathless Mary had caught up with him. "Don't, Bill!" she panted, placing a hand upon his arm. But too late, for the ball of knotted anger in his guts had spewed out into a red mist and he lashed out with his boots.

"Come out! Or I'll kick the bleedin' door down!" he yelled. The sound of grating metal as the key slowly turned, brought him to a halt. With fists lowered, he stood stock-still when the door was slowly opened a crack, and within its dark chink a shaggy-moustached, pale face appeared.

Silence.

Then all hell was let loose.

"You bastard!" Bill lunged towards the face and, before it could retreat into the darkness, his hand shot up and, scragging him out, disposed of him by tossing him onto the street like a dead rat. "Sara?" he whispered, peeping into the room. He was answered by a whimpering. His eyes, not accustomed to the gloom, searched around frantically. The shaft of light when he opened the door fully, slowly crept around the walls towards the darkest recess. Then he saw her.

"Gawd, gel! What's he done to you?" He stepped gently towards his beloved and tenderly opened his arms. Slowly and painfully Sara, black with the beating her father had given her, crawled into them. Bill rocked her to-and-fro and vowed then and there to always provide for her, and to do what was right by her.

Mary had joined them and, handing Sara over to her, Bill silently crossed the room, picked up the poker and went outside.

With dignity he faced her father. "Do that again," he quietly stated, stepping closer until the two faces, one haggard and anguished, the other contorted in fear, almost touched. Watson winced as Bill raised the poker high then, lowering it, snapped, "And I'll kill you..."

The silence was broken by the chinking of the poker bouncing over the pavement.

Bill kept his promise and, as soon as he found a tiny terrace just off Lawrence Street to rent, he brought Sara to safety and they were married.

At regular intervals Sara produced bonny, bouncing babies, the small house gladly stretching to accommodate the ever-growing brood. Oh, how Bill craved a son! But it wasn't to be, and over eight years, as his lovely wife presented him with one beautiful girl after another, Bill lamented long and loud, "Oh, no...not another split-arse!"

But, girls or no, this man did his duty by his family; for he'd promised they would survive against all-odds. He did his duty well and to the best of his ability, for he was king of the wee abode crammed full-up to the roof and bulging at the seams with women. Or so he thought; little realising that his wriggling and giggling kingdom, of which he fancied himself 'Cock-of-the-walk' was, in reality, of a wilful and very determined matriarchal rule.

When Bill was taken on by York Council as a 'Refuse-disposal operative', he thought himself very fortunate. To his way of thinking it was not only regular, it was also very gainful and heaven-blessed employment – for not only did he get to empty the wheelie-bins, he also got access to the tip on Foss Island's Road. Dross to the eyes of some, was a godsend in Bill's, for it ensured one more day's survival. From here many a treasure became ensconced in the deep pockets of the Parka he'd found whilst skip-diving one day.

The discovery of such wondrous items fired up his zest for life and he would bound in (blissfully unaware, or craftily unheeding of Sara's chunterings behind his back, "'As 'e bin' bin-divin' again! What rubbish 'as the muck-tub brought home this time? I don't want no more bloody rubbish!"), pat his pockets and proclaim, "Unsight, or unseen!"

Although each and every girl was loved equally, the truth of the matter – though he would never admit it – was that he had a favourite amongst them. Only one of the eight had been blessed with red locks and cheeky, vivid-blue eyes, and being a bit of a tomboy, was the son he'd never had. So, it was her he'd singled-out to give boxing lessons to. Her who'd got his fondest nickname. And her, he knew, who was in dire need of some trainers.

And so it was, after weeks of relentlessly scouring the tip and delving and diving into every available bin and skip, that Bill bounded in as ever and made his proclamation for all to hear. Ensuring himself of the full attention of one-and-all, he then, very deftly, from the bowels of a pocket, produced a Nike trainer. "Try that for size, Rice-arse!" he said, swelling with pride.

Grinning, she put her foot in it. "Aw, Dad. It's a bit big!"

"You'll grow into it," was his swift reply.

Her blue eyes watched expectantly whilst he slowly slid his hand into his other pocket.

"Stop tormenting the bairn and gerrit out, Bill!" Sara ordered.

All breaths were held as slowly he drew the contents out. "Aw, Dad!" wailed his pride-and-joy. "It's not the same brand...and it's a different colour!"

"Well, walk fast – an' no-one'll notice, an' if they do, they'll think there's summat-up with their eyes," was the retort.

"But, Dad...it's a left one an'all..."

"The bleedin' warmth of your foot'll bend it into shape..."

"Never mind, Honey," Sara whispered behind Bill's back to the now blubbing Rice-arse. "When the dirty devil's back's turned, we'll sneak 'em back in't bin..."

Further weeks of vigilant back-breaking rootling around the tip eventually brought their reward. Wary glances were exchanged amongst the womenfolk as they eyed the bulging pocket and the fateful words were declared. Sara pursed her lips and chuntered, "'Ere, 'as 'e bin' bin-divin' again! I've told 'im, I don't want no more rubbish!"

"Oh, but this is an 'eirloom, gel," said Bill. "I won't be surprised if it's not worth a bob or two," he cajoled, sliding his arm deep-down inside his pocket. He paused, ensuring everyone was watching, then produced, like a magician from a hat, a large vase. "Ain't it a beauty?" he proudly asked, blowing it.

"Don't blow muck off in 'ere!" yelled an unconvinced Sara.

"'Ere, Rice-arse. Go an' wash it." A thorough scrubbing quickly revealed that beneath the muck it wasn't too bad. "There y'are, gel, what could be nicer than that, eh?" he grinned.

Sara just couldn't understand what all the fuss was over a blob vase, that no-one in their right minds gave house room to nowadays – except Bill, that is, who gave it pride of place on their shelf.

Two days later, when she was sure that he was well away from home, Sara sneaked the vase out and it went the same way as the mobile phone as-big-as-a-brick had gone – deep down inside her bin. A sigh of relief went up the next day when it was emptied.

"Unsight, or unseen!" announced Bill a week later.

"What you got? More junk?" chuntered Sara.

He waited as all eyes turned. Slowly, a large vase was produced. "The pair!" he exclaimed.

"Wh...at?" asked a bemused Sara.

"I've found the matching one to our 'eirloom...!"

"You. Daft. Sod. Bill!"

"What you all giggling about? Come on, Rice-arse...tell me..."

York held its breath in anticipation of a new century. It blew in like a razzamatazzick gale, and fizzled out quicker than the fireworks, like a fart in a draught, as people realised that nothing had changed – except the date. Sara hadn't been impressed by it all and still clung tenaciously to her fierce pride and honesty, for while you had that, at least you had something. Bill doggedly kept his promise, and had always provided, and done what was right, for his lovely Sara. This was uppermost in his mind one day as he set off for work.

St. Lawrence Church had been locked up for years for public safety. Bill passed it every day on his way to the tip. On this particular morning, by special request, it had been unlocked for a funeral and, curiosity getting the better of him, he went inside. He gazed around at its peeling splendour. There was something about its dignified, poverty-stricken air that he empathized with. "There y'ar, you poor bugger," echoed his whisper as, upon leaving, he donated his last pound to its fabric fund.

That night after work he slunk into the house. One deep pocket of his Parka concealed – judging by the bulge and how lop-sided his coat was – one extremely heavy object.

Sara looked on, smiling and waiting for his usual banter. She was puzzled when he didn't utter one single word. The girls watched, intrigued by his furtive air, as first he closed the living-room door, then went over to the window. After checking that there was no one outside in their backyard, he crossed over to the table, then looked over his shoulder before sliding his hand into his pocket. As his arm vanished deep down into its depths, he paused. Turning his head towards his wife, he quietly said, "Sara?"

The girls knew then that this was important, for he rarely talked quietly and only gave their mam her proper name in times of considerable graveness.

"Sara," he continued, "what would you most like in all the world...if you could 'ave it?"

"Don't talk so daft, Bill!" Sara retorted.

"No, I mean it. What would you like?" he asked.

The girls' mouths hung open, looking first at one parent, then the other. Their mam was bewildered. Their dad could hardly conceal his excitement.

"What 'ave you been up to, Bill?" Sara asked softly, drying her hands on a tea-towel.

He eagerly wrestled with the contents of his pocket then, with difficulty, withdrew it. All stared pocket-wards. The room held a hushed silence, no one daring to breath as nine pairs of eyes followed his every move. Easing the article out, he steadied it in both hands and placed it on the table top. "Just name it, gel, and it's yours!" he said, grinning and gesturing towards the table.

The girls looked at their mam then quickly back to the table.

"Aw, Dad. It's on'y an old tin box," one sister hissed disappointedly, then mumbled, "An' not a very good 'un at that...it's all dented...an' rusty!"

"Chub-a-bleedin' row!" commanded Bill.

Silence fell, the tension becoming almost palpable. Sara, not uttering a single word throughout the palaver, stood stock-still, trying to think how an old, dented, tin box could grant you any wish you wanted. Finally, in exasperation, she shook her head.

Slowly the stiff lid was prised open with an old, pointed knife. Its contents made all eyes stick out like chapel hat-pegs. Silence. Then an "Ooh..." filled the air. Then bedlam. All but Sara started babbling. There was leaping and screaming, whooping and clapping, for all the world to hear.

For the box was full to the brim with what looked like old gold coins.

"God above! Where did they come from?" asked a frightened Sara, suddenly becoming animated and drawing closer to him.

Silence fell. All stared at Bill.

"Off the bleedin' tip. I were pokin' 'round a bit an' I came across them."

"Oh...Bill. They're not ours!"

"Course they bleedin' well are. Finders-keepers in my book!"

Silenced by their loyalty to both parents, the girls risked a quiet nod.

"You daft devil, you! Do you think somebody threw 'em away 'cos they didn't want 'em anymore?"

"No, gel – but it'll teach 'em to be more careful in future!"

"Bill. You tek 'em back this minute!"

"Can't. They will 'ave all gone home by now."

"Well tomorro' then. First thing in't mornin'. You tek 'em back!" shouted Sara, becoming agitated.

"You could have anything you want, gel...just for the askin'," wheedled Bill. "You'd never want for anything – ever again."

"'Cept peace of mind."

"I promised I'd provide for you. Now here's the best, and probably only chance I'll ever have!"

Sara's voice trembled as she too remembered. "You also promised you'd do what's right by me. And this isn't right...I'd never rest easy in me bed. What pleasure would I get from always having to look over me shoulder?"

"We could flit."

"You can't run forever from your own conscience!" Gentler now she said, "'Ow could I enjoy 'em...when they're not mine to enjoy?"

They faced one another, an air of defiance between them, neither backing down, like a pair of fighting cocks trapped in a pit of promises, poverty and pride.

Eventually, Sara broke their silence. "Promise me, before you decide what you're gonna do with 'em, you'll think over what I've said..."

Bill slowly blinked, then nodded once.

Later, lying four to a bed, the girls contemplated their fortunes.

Sara was very quiet the next morning, staring into space whilst shaking cornflakes along the line of bowls.

"Has Dad gone to work?" one daughter asked.

"Aye," was Sara's quiet reply.

"And...has he...tekken...?" she ventured.

Not knowing Bill's decision, Sara shrugged and shook the box faster.

The day crawled by for everyone. The slam of the door as Bill came home at teatime made everyone jump, their hearts in their mouths. Sara was busily buttering bread. When she heard the door she stopped and looked up. "Well?" she asked, clutching the knife so tight that her knuckles turned white.

The girls gathered close, watching and waiting.

"I took it back," he answered, his voice flat.

Sara heaved a big sigh as the weight of the world was removed from her shoulders, "And?" she asked, relieved.

He paused to check he had his audience's undivided attention. "I went straight to the manager's office, just like you said," he shot a glance at Sara. "There was a fat, toffee-nosed git, talking to him. He was enquiring about a box which..." Bill stuck his nose in the air, and mimicking the man's voice continued, "...'Thrown out in error'."

"Stop actin' daft, Bill and gerron wi' it!"

He shook his head, "'Ow the 'ell do you throw summat like that away by mistake? That's what I want to know!"

"It's not for the likes of us to know," Sara stated wisely. "And sometimes it's best not to know," she added. "Now, will you gerron wi' it!"

"Well," he continued, "I asked if this was the one. He snatched it from me an', in a flash, tussled the lid open and checked it was all there. 'It seems to be intact,' he said and put his big, fat, sweaty hand into his swanky, suit pocket. He brings out some loose change and as he sorts through it, I thought, 'I'm alright here, he's gonna reward me!' Then he said – in that plum-throated voice of his, all nasal-like – 'Here you are, my good man.' And do you know what he gave me for all my trouble?"

Gawping, the girls shook their heads.

"Fifty bleedin' pence!" With boisterousness returning, he continued, "If it weren't for fear of being sacked, I'd've asked the git if he could touch his toes...an' if he had've, I'd a' shoved that bleedin' coin – bevelled-edges an' all – right up his... 'Ere, what're you lot laughin' at?"

Upon hearing Bill's raucous laughter joining with the girls', Sara's heart gladdened; she smiled, then started to cut the soft-boiled eggs in half. Her hands moved deftly as each dome was swiftly stood upon its point, preventing the spillage of their precious half-yolks, so ensuring that there was enough to share around her household of women and Bill, of whom she was so quietly proud.

The Clerk's Tale

David Darton

"Wayte what thyng we may nat lightly have,

Therafter wol we crie al day and crave.

Forbede us thyng, and that desiren we;

Preesse on us faste, and thanne wol we fle."

The Wife of Bath's Prologue

"Jane! We haven't seen you here for a while," the barman said.

"No, I haven't been back to York for a while. You remember the Russian I was dating? Mikhail, the biochemist from the University that I was so proud of snaring?" she laughed. "Well, he got a job in Manchester and I went with him. He's doing really well – he heads up the forensic lab for the Greater Manchester Police."

"What brings you back then?"

"Oh, I'm not staying, I'm just here for a wedding tomorrow. Mikhail and I had a bit of a row when I left, so I really need to get back straight away."

"So, have you got a tale to add to the evening?"

Jane took a sip of her drink. "Well, I suppose it is a sort of a tale that's on my mind right now. I'll tell it in return for another of these." She emptied her glass and raised her eyebrows at the barman.

"Manchester hasn't improved you," he observed.

It's about this woman I know: Sharon; a pretty woman, slim and dark, although the first day I met her she looked *really* rough. That wasn't unusual in those early days. She told me later that it was down to the bad start each day. Her daughter, Kate, had just started going to a day-care nursery and didn't want Sharon to leave her there. Apparently she would scream and scream. Mrs. Hadley, her teacher, would reassure Sharon that Kate would be okay once she had gone. But Sharon didn't really believe her and would wait until the last possible moment before leaving. Then she would race down Priory Street and into Micklegate. At the bottom of Micklegate, she would rush into the Ladies on Toft Green to straighten herself up. In an insurance company you had to look smart, even if you were just processing boring application forms. She would generally be only a couple of minutes late and the other girls in the open-plan office wouldn't yet have settled down. Sharon knew a few of their names, but as she only ever arrived just before work started and worked through her break (so that she could leave promptly after her half-day's work), she had not really made any friends. That's what made it worse. All she could hear in her head was Kate's anguish. Kate was all she had.

She rarely allowed herself to remember how she had rejected the baby at first. When she did, she was filled with an unbearable shame.

After a few weeks, it seemed to be coming right. Both she and Kate were settling into a routine. The doctors had explained that due to her learning disability, Kate would find change difficult. But the last three days her protests seemed more token; she stopped crying before Sharon left the nursery. Apparently, she was relating well to one of the volunteer assistants who had been assigned to her as a sort of mentor.

The insurance work was tedious though, even for Sharon. Really boring. And being bored was a problem. A low boredom threshold was one of the things that got her hooked on drugs in the first place. There were moments in this friendless, mind-numbing office when she found herself craving the rush, even if the physical demand was not as acute as it had once been.

Sharon couldn't even break the boredom with chat. She was embarrassed talking to the other girls, most of whom were younger than she was. Their talk was of 'going out' and their latest fancies. She couldn't afford to do anything other than shop for essentials and watch the box long into the evening. And who would understand what it was like having a young child so dependent on you? She still found it difficult talking about Kate's problems. After all, they were all Sharon's fault. Better not to talk.

After a while she began to open up to me. I was older and a bit more worldly-wise than the rest of the girls. I took over from Sharon for the afternoon shift and we got into the habit of having a coffee together in the canteen, while Sharon told me of any queries she hadn't been able to deal with during the morning. She was always quite hyper and checking her watch to make sure that she left in time to pick-up Kate. I eventually persuaded Sharon to bring Kate to the pub after work once a week and we had some longer talks, loosened up with a couple of drinks.

She told me that while Kate was awake, it stopped her thinking too much. Sharon could immerse herself in her child; the slightly lop-sided smiles that were so hard to elicit, made her insides do cartwheels. Sharon would laugh with Kate and hold her tight. But it wasn't clear to me who was providing comfort to whom.

The first hour after Kate went to bed wasn't too bad. Sharon would allow herself the first of only two cigarettes she had each day and then spend some time cleaning the small flat, which by the end of every evening was spotless to the point of fanaticism. But then it could get difficult. The telly helped. But she knew deep down that she would always miss that release from anxiety that came when she shot up; for her, as important as the exhilaration that also came. She had strategies to resist going back to the stuff, but somehow it had become harder now that she had accidentally seen someone dealing on the estate and knew where the shit could be obtained. As she got more tired and the temptation got greater, she would go to bed and just look at Kate. The love she felt overwhelmed her. There seemed to be some kind of spiritual link, even when they weren't touching.

Sharon would resist sleep for as long as possible, knowing that the flashbacks would come when she did finally begin to doze off.

Most of her drug-saturated years were lost to her. The images that did randomly flash into her mind were mostly of dirt. Grime on walls; stains, or worse, on carpets. People seemed to drift by in a haze of motionless faces, punctuated every now and then by sharp expressions of joy or pain as needles entered, pills were swallowed or penises – countless penises without personalities attached – exploded inside her or inside someone across the room.

Sharon would try and escape the cruelly clear recollections of these moments with romantic memories of Kate's father. His was a face of rare animation; of thought and of care, in amongst the hopelessness. He was the one who left to find a way out, who would come back for her. She knew this, because they must have both been special to create Kate, a special child, signalled by the bright red diamond birthmark below, and to the right, of her belly button. Special, even if Sharon's drug-racked body had left their love child short of something.

The trouble was that part of her always knew that Kate's dad was just another one of the anonymous penises.

I found myself beginning to care about Sharon and what happened to her. She was one of those people who had that effect on you, pitiful though she was – in many ways. When I decided to leave York, it was the idea of not being there for her that worried me the most.

I convinced myself that it wouldn't really matter because I would always keep in touch; and things seemed to be going better for Sharon anyway. Kate seemed more settled, either through the skills of Mrs. Hadley or the one-to-one attention of her mentor-volunteer.

I also consoled myself with the thought that at least my replacement, Frank, seemed okay. He was one of these idealist types, doing right-on things like caring for people and the environment in the morning, and then working in the afternoon. He was too earnest for me, but he was friendly.

After I left, I realized that Sharon saw Frank differently. With his long, lanky hair he was one of those no-hopers from her past. He might have a part time job, but he didn't really have any actual responsibility, did he?

"You know," said Sharon with disgust, "he even admitted to me, in that horrible drawl of his, that he couldn't concentrate during one of our handovers because he had seen an old friend that morning and shared a spliff with him." Sharon despised these middle-class dropouts; wrecking their lives through laziness and drugs, when they had had all that advantage to start with.

In the weeks after I left, it was clear that Frank was obviously getting to her.

"You know," she said in one of our frequent phone calls, "he keeps looking at me in *that* way. Like he knows what I want and he is the one to give it to me. He starts off those conversations. You know the ones. When guys look at you with a sort of fake intensity. 'Do you mind if we talk about something serious?' That sort of crap. How dare he? I don't even know him. What makes him think I would fall for that old approach? I cut him off straight away, I can tell you. I mean, what makes him think I care enough to want to 'talk seriously'?" Her voice dripped with contempt.

I could tell it was never going to be better between them. To her, he was just like all those men from before. She even said that he began appearing in her nightmares. Not just having his way with her, but telling her how stupid she was and what a waster she was. It was clear she was going to have to rely on me still, even at a distance.

But I could not be there for her every day. She thought Frank was a complete arsehole and hadn't got any better at getting to know the others in the office. She had no one to let off steam with each day. No one to remind her how well she was doing; from a complete mess to a decent mother in little over a year; Kate no longer in care; her with some purpose in life.

So she found herself bottling everything up again and retreating into self-doubt, and even self-loathing. I suppose as I got into things in Manchester, our phone calls did get less frequent. Otherwise, I might have picked-up the danger signals earlier. The last time I spoke to her before it all went pear-shaped, she told me that she was even finding herself tense with Kate.

Most of the time, Kate holding on to her, cuddling her, playing with her, were the most joyous moments of the day. Even if Kate's development was slower than most other kids, the progress she made, the increasing frequency of smiles and happiness, validated Sharon's life. But there were times too when Kate's demands felt – what's the word? – oppressive; too needy. Sharon admitted to me in one phone call that she would push Kate away, sometimes very forcefully. At first, it would last only a moment.

"It's horrible, Jane. Kate's little face looks puzzled and hurt at the same time, and I just have to go to her. I feel so ashamed."

But Sharon's rejection of Kate became increasingly prolonged, particularly in the early evening. She would close her eyes hard shut as the puzzled hurt on Kate's face turned to sobbing. She would cover her ears, or shut the door to the bathroom and light up. And just wait...and wait. Willing the child away.

Of course, the remorse afterwards became more and more intense. I would have Sharon on the phone for hours, in tears. Mikhail would get quite irritated. I didn't really know how to help her and Sharon didn't know how to make it up to Kate. She felt really terrible. Yet it didn't stop it happening the next time.

Sharon's dislike of herself increased. She needed something to reduce the tensions, to get rid of the fear and self-doubt that were beginning to take over her head.

When it did all blow up, it happened real quick. The first I knew was the phone call from a hospital bed. When she was in need, I was always the one Sharon called. She was a bit incoherent, but I gradually pieced it together.

One lunchtime, Frank hadn't turned up to take over from her at work. She had waited as long as she could before reporting it. Then she had had to run. She struggled up the hill at the bottom of Micklegate, already out of breath as she passed the old church and still had half a mile to go. Turning into Priory Street, she could see Mrs Hadley scanning the street.

But it wasn't Sharon that Mrs Hadley was looking for. It was Kate.

"She was with Francis; you know, the volunteer I told you about. I asked him to stay on a bit and meet you, like we discussed."

'Francis? What sort of name's that for a bloke?' she thought irrelevantly, still out of breath and not yet to grips with the situation.

"They were in the yard – and you know we always have the gate locked. Well, they've gone and I don't know what to do. Should I call the police?"

"Christ, you're the one whose supposed to know what to

do," yelled Sharon, the fear welling up inside her turning to anger.

"There they are," Mrs Hadley said suddenly. Sharon turned and in the distance saw Kate holding on to a man's hand. Presumably Francis. They got nearer.

"Christ, no. It can't be," screamed Sharon. "Bloody hell, it's bloody Frank." She started to run down the street towards them.

"You frigging deceiving turd," Sharon yelled, snatching Kate away from him. Then her fury reached a point beyond control and she lashed out, hitting him first in the face and then ineffectually in the stomach.

"No, Ma. No. No." Kate freed herself from Sharon and went to Frank, holding onto him tightly.

"No! No! You're mine," Sharon screamed. She grabbed at Kate and yanked her hard. Kate stumbled and fell. She looked up at Sharon in fear, tears streaming down her face. And, in that moment, Kate chose Frank. Getting to her feet, she turned and reached around his legs for comfort. Sharon raised her eyes from Kate. Bizarrely, Frank had pulled his trousers half down at one side and was pointing at a red patch on his skin, below, and to the right, of his belly button. It was too much for Sharon. So Frank hadn't just come into her nightmares. Christ, he was there all the time. One of the anonymous penises. She turned on Kate.

"Okay. Fine," she said to the sobbing four-year-old, gritting her teeth, unable to contain her rage and her fear. Then to Frank, "Go on then, you have her. She obviously prefers you and no doubt you're better for her than me." She didn't know where the power came from, but she ran and stumbled all the way back to the estate. She was useless. It had all been a sham.

The dealer was in his normal place. She pulled what money she had from her purse. She didn't even know what it cost any more. The dealer took it all. In return for a syringe, as well as the stuff. Sharon didn't even wait to get in the flat. The pain of the needle was exquisite. Suddenly it seemed sort of okay. Then, very quickly, much more than okay. She would sort things out. Tomorrow.

Sharon made it to the front door. Got the key in. Got the door open before she collapsed into the flat and started to vomit over the sparkling clean floor, her legs sticking out into the stairwell.

Her only visitor, apart from me, was Frank. He arrived, with slightly bedraggled flowers, and I left them to it.

It was all very simple really. Frank told me that he had been on drink mainly when he first met Sharon about five years previously. He smoked the odd joint, but never took the really hard shit the rest of them were on. He and Sharon had made it together a few times in the squat they had both lived in briefly. In the rare moments she was half lucid, he liked her. It had been a while since he had bothered to have a woman more than once and he wanted to take things further. But after a while he fully understood how far gone she really was. Self-preservation kicked in. Frank left.

He sorted himself out and went on to do a social work degree in York, including a placement at the nursery in Priory Street. Afterwards, he had gone back there as a volunteer and started to get friendly with Kate. You can just imagine the shock when he saw the diamond birthmark – close enough to his own to make him wonder. So, one day he had waited and seen Sharon pick her up. Then he knew. He couldn't believe his luck in finding them. But then, he had made the 20-mile transfer from Leeds to the relative tranquillity of York, to sort himself out. He supposed it was no surprise that Sharon had done so too. After all, he knew that there had been something special in her, even back then.

Frank started following Sharon to work. He laughed about her always being in a perpetual state of being late. It made her easy to follow – she never had time to look behind her.

When the job at the insurance company came up, he couldn't resist applying for it.

"I needed a job to tide me over while I looked for a permanent one in social work. And, anyway, it was time to let Sharon see me."

But then he had two shocks in succession. First, he found he was actually job-sharing with her. Second, he found she did not know him.

"I kept waiting for her to recognize me. I thought I must have meant something to her; that she would remember me. I tried to start serious conversations that might lead to me being able to tell her. But she kept cutting me off."

Mrs Hadley wanted him to meet Sharon. He couldn't really keep putting it off. But Sharon was showing no warmth to him at all at work, in fact, barely disguised dislike.

He knew from his training how wrong it would be to confront her with Kate present, so he planned to come and see her early that day at work and tell her all about it. With this on his mind, he was finding it difficult being at the nursery. So when Kate wanted to see his house, he gave in, breaking all the rules. After all, he thought, it could do no harm. The flat his parents were renting for him was close by, in the new development behind Micklegate. And after all, he *was* her dad.

But Kate had dawdled, excited about leaving the nursery. Then she had wanted the toilet. Then she wouldn't leave and the timing had all gone haywire.

And he was sorry.

Sharon told him to piss off.

But she had to listen. She was stuck in hospital and she knew better than to discharge herself – it would have been straight back to the drugs. And Kate would have to go into care. But she told Frank what she thought of him.

The next day he came with washed and cut hair. Although Sharon had severe doubts at first, she gradually opened up to him. Frank became Francis. And I became irrelevant, not needed any more.

Sharon realised that Francis was far from a loser. And he did seem to care. Maybe her romanticisation of Kate's dad was not so far off. And he understood her. Kept telling her how well she had done against the odds. That he had been in that scene too. That he understood.

They came over to see us in Manchester about three months ago. I'd had nothing but a couple of minutes' rushed phone call, every couple of months for the last year. Not like it was when she needed me, hey? But Francis had finally asked her to marry him and she wanted me to be her chief bridesmaid. I'm a sucker for all that stuff, so here I am, for the great day tomorrow. It's at the church in Micklegate that she used to pass every day between the nursery and work, with Francis following secretly behind. Kate is a bridesmaid with me. Mrs Hadley is the maid of honour.

"Well, it *is* nice to have a story with a happy ending," said the barman.

"Mmmm," said Jane pensively.

"Well, it is, isn't it?"

"The trouble is, it might not be. It's up to me, I suppose. You see, it's those birthmarks on Francis and Kate. When she was upset with Francis at the beginning, unsure whether to like him or not, she described the birthmarks to me; told me that they are not really the same – just in a similar position. In fact,

Frank's is just a slight, ill-defined reddening of the skin. Now, of course, Sharon is convinced that Francis is Kate's dad and doesn't think about that any more, but it kept nagging at me. I couldn't bear not knowing. So I persuaded Mikhail to do some tests on the traces of the cups Kate and Francis used when they came over, to find out if Francis really is the father. You see, I've always had this thing about knowing the truth."

"Or is it because you're jealous and she ignores you now," said a man further down the bar.

"No, it's not," Jane snapped. "That's what Mikhail said. Mikhail thought that Sharon had asked me to get him to do the tests. When he found out it was just me, well, he went ballistic. That's why Mikhail isn't here. He doesn't think I should give her this." She pulled a sealed envelope out of her bag.

"But doesn't Kate have a right to know if Francis is really her dad?"

The Actress's Tale

Sam Haward

"For paramour I loved hire first er thow.

What wiltow seyen? Thou woost nat yet now

Wheither she be a womman or goddesse!"

The Knight's Tale

Patience was born on 18th October 1975, in San Diego. She starred in her first commercial, advertising baby shampoo, aged two. At seven, she gained a regular part in 'The Bold and the Beautiful'. She checked into her first rehab clinic aged fourteen, more as a career move than to resolve any underlying psychological problems, where she lost her virginity to a recovering director who promptly cast her in his next film. She joined the A-list following the unexpected success of the thriller 'Terminal Romance', but was demoted when the biopic of Vera Lynn bombed. She regained her status in 2000, when she found her forte as the queen of romantic comedies. Currently unmarried, she has been romantically linked to a number of Hollywood actors. But then, you shouldn't believe everything you read in the papers.

This story serves as a salutary reminder that some worlds are just not supposed to collide. It's quite scary to see how York folk's instinctive common-sense and natural generosity could be so quickly cast aside in pursuance of the cult of celebrity. I know it can all be put down to the temporary madness brought on by Ascot week, but frankly that's no excuse. York folk should know better.

The story starts with Patience Harling's plane soaring into the night sky above New York City. Truth be told, although she behaved as though it was her plane – patronising the stewardesses and the like – it was actually a commercial flight. Her film company refused to fly her to London in a private jet, so she sulked about this for a week, before she fired one of her assistants and felt better. Since Patience was Hollywood's latest diva-in-chief, this was only natural and appropriate behaviour. You must have heard of her. She's appeared in all the successful tear-jerkers over the past few years – her fiery Californian temperament setting the screen ablaze. You will have seen her on some magazine cover, flaunting her curvaceous sun-kissed body and her trademark flame-blonde hair.

"Excuse me, darling. Will you please stop making eyes at the air hostess and put your mind to ordering drinks. I'll have a large Bailey's," said Patience.

Miguel immediately jumped to attention. As Patience's PA, he was well aware that his responsibility was to pander to her every whim. He didn't have particularly good organisational skills, but made up for this by being an extremely beautiful Puerto Rican who had modelled for Calvin Klein and therefore added to the overall glamour of Patience's lifestyle. Miguel understood that unemployment was but a temper-tantrum away, so he caught the stewardess's eye and, with a single glance, simultaneously ordered a round of drinks and a rendezvous in one of the rest-rooms for later. Miguel was an active member of the Mile High Club and never watched an in-flight movie if he didn't have to.

Sitting next to Patience was her current flame – the heart-throb actor Dack Dakers. He had become an overnight celebrity after playing the plucky centurion in 'Hadrian's Wall', although the fact that he spent most of the movie showing off his gym-trained muscles goes a long way towards explaining his current fan-base. He certainly couldn't act for toffee. Their whirlwind romance began at the Cannes Film Festival, but their busy schedules meant they had hardly seen each other since. As a recovering sex-aholic, Dack did not find the infrequency of their meetings to be at all helpful.

Patience's next starring role was to be 'The American Princess', a rom-com by numbers in which a charismatic, yet vulnerable, American nanny wins the heart of an English prince. To prepare for the role, she had booked herself on a whistle-stop tour of English high society: Harrods, Wimbledon, the ballet... To her chagrin, tea with the Queen had apparently been impossible to arrange; however Patience was instead to meet the talk-show hosts Richard and Judy, who she was told had similar status. The tour was to start off with a week at the Races – Royal Ascot. She found it confusing that this was to take place in somewhere called York, but put it down to the quaint and amusing way that the English went about things. She wasn't to know that this was a temporary arrangement while the usual racecourse was redeveloped. She was looking forward to it, as any event requiring an entire day's hat shopping had to be worthwhile.

Miguel was slightly nervous about the impending visit to York. He was responsible for booking their accommodation, which was no easy task since all the hotel rooms had gone months before. Patience had said that she didn't expect to have to travel far and that it had to have, "some of that authentic historical crap", so that she could get into character. With some relief he had found something fitting the bill on the internet.

"Delightful, authentic, York residence. Part of the city's rich cultural history as a former home of chocolate workers. Racecourse stands at top of street. Three bedrooms. Only £5000 for the week."

Miguel snapped it up, making the logical assumption that only the very best houses would be right next to the Racecourse. This, of course, just goes to show how important local knowledge really is.

A certain excitement abounded in Curzon Terrace. Pete and Angela's next-door neighbours had just gone to stay with the in-laws for a week, and speculation was running rife as to who might be moving in instead. The local residents had already been tantalised by the appearance of two actors from EastEnders at the window of number 75; a rather famous page three model who appeared to be sporting an enhanced cleavage had been seen at number 52; and a posse of obligatory ex-Big Brother contestants had been spotted nipping into number 7.

Most impressively of all so far, Richard Whitely, host of the cult TV gameshow 'Countdown', had moved into number 56. In the eyes of everyone on the street, this was quite a coup. Richard had near-iconic status amongst the local residents, indeed throughout the country, although quite why this should be true was always a bit of a puzzle. Richard himself was a middle-aged and rather unassuming chap, with a sense of humour somewhat akin to that of a genial uncle. However, at 3.15pm weekdays, those residents of Curzon Terrace who didn't have the misfortune to work, chiefly the retired and student populations, gathered around their TV sets for their daily fix of word-play and mental arithmetic. And now he was living on their street! Perhaps it was no wonder that the excitement of Ascot week was getting far too much for everyone.

"So do you think anyone famous will turn up next door?" wondered Angela excitedly.

Pete was reading the local paper. The headline stated that there was controversy about the closure of the bus-lanes to make way for the Royal Procession. Apparently one councillor (certainly Labour) was quoted as saying that they should use the Park and Ride like everyone else.

"Maybe. They'd better not make too much of a racket, or I'll be having words," said Pete.

Pete and Angela were just coming up to their first wedding anniversary. Pete was thirty-two and worked as an engineer on the Railways. His dress-sense was, at best, scruffy and he was beginning to acquire his own personal beer keg round his midriff. Angela was a petite twenty-nine year-old who worked as a secretary for DEFRA (the Department of Environment, Food and Rural Affairs, for non-Yorkers).

"I'd better get my hair done," she continued. "I think my

highlights are beginning to fade." Angela was blonde, but only with assistance from the hairdresser.

"You had them done last bloody week! Good grief, woman. If anyone famous does move in next door, they're not going to be talking to the likes of us. They'll be hob-nobbing with the likes of Tara Mara Wotsit."

"You don't know that. They must get sick of meeting all those celebrity types. They'd probably love to meet real people like us. We'd be a breath of fresh air."

Angela was nothing if not optimistic, but had spent far too much time reading 'Cosmopolitan' for her own good.

At half past three, a white limousine pulled into Curzon Terrace and proceeded to drive up the narrow street, knocking off three wing mirrors in the process. From the inside, there came the sound of raised voices.

"This can't be right. You must have got the wrong address. All the houses are joined together! It's like visiting the third frigging world!"

A few net curtains twitched and a number of people came out onto the street to see what was happening.

"We can't stay here," said Patience, "We'll have to book into a hotel!"

"But they're all booked. I've already tried," wailed Miguel.

A furious Patience slammed the limousine door and marched into their new home wearing dark glasses and a hastily improvised head-scarf. Dack took the time to wave to the gathering crowd, but was disappointed to hear someone muttering, "Wasn't he in that band, Boyzone?"

The house had a typical terrace layout, with a small front room, slightly larger lounge and galley kitchen looking over a small yard. The décor was a horrific blend of flowery wallpaper and garishly painted woodchip.

Patience finally let her feelings rip:

"Just what kind of squalid excuse for a house is this? My God, 'Hello' would have a field day. No-one will want to visit us the whole week!"

Timing being everything, at this moment there came a knock at the door, followed by a hesitant call of 'hello'. In came Angela, with a reluctant Pete trailing behind.

"Hi. I'm Angela. This is Pete. We're from next door. You are staying for Ascot, aren't you? Have you come far?" she burbled helplessly.

"New York," replied a somewhat stunned Patience.

"Oh. Isn't that funny. Now you are in old York. Or rather Ye Olde Yorke!" she said chattily, "So are you famous?"

This final question stopped Patience in her tracks. She was aghast at the thought that she had not been recognized. Miguel quickly tried to regain some kudos.

"Is she famous? My God! This is Patience Harling. Star of 'Angel for a day'!"

"I know you. Weren't you once engaged to Ben Affleck?"

"No," snapped Patience, "That was someone else."

"Sorry, but we've had a long journey. We'd like to freshen up," said Dack, bored of the conversation.

"Yes, of course," said Angela, "We just thought we'd say hello. We're throwing a little party tomorrow night to celebrate Ascot week. Just us and a few of the neighbours. Do say you'll come. Everyone would love to meet you."

"Fine!" said Patience, followed by, "Jeez, I thought they'd never leave," when they had gone.

"You're not really going to their party are you?" Miguel asked.

"Hell no!" replied Patience, "But I had to get rid of them somehow."

The next day the Race meeting began. Suffice it to say that it passed off with all the pageantry, dignity, and ceremony one would expect. Crowds of the rich and famous got off their faces on cheap champagne and lost lots of money on the horses; all the time resplendent in their various designer garments, equal in total to the budget of a small developing country. The Queen and Duke of Edinburgh, for their part, quite enjoyed the occasion. A visit to York made a welcome change, what with the procession passing the Minster and Roman walls, even if the Queen was rather peeved that there wasn't sufficient time to visit Betty's Tea Room.

That evening, Angela waited anxiously for her guests to arrive. Word had quickly, and satisfyingly, spread amongst the neighbours and quite a crowd was gathered in her lounge, all curiously awaiting the arrival of a couple of Hollywood megastars. Angela was unsure what was appropriate, so had fallen back on the usual spread of dips, crisps, sausage rolls and quiche (although she did buy this from the 'finest' range). By nine o'clock they still hadn't arrived and, for the neighbours, jealousy of Angela's (over-stated) fraternisation with the celebrity classes was now turning to glee that no-one appeared to be turning up at all. As it turned out, Patience, Dack and Miguel had arrived back next door some time ago, but a fateful combination of jet-lag, alcohol and social antipathy meant they had just crashed out asleep.

By ten o'clock, Angela had given up. She felt furious and humiliated and decided to move to plan B. Enlisting those remaining guests, she asked the burning question:

"Right then! How are we going to get our own back?"

Angela and Pete's next actions were distinctly out of character. However, you had to hand it to them. Once they decided upon their plan of revenge, they executed it with the precision of a military campaign.

Early the next morning, Patience awoke with a start to find a man (Mike from number 24) on a ladder cleaning the bedroom window.

"Morning love!" he called out cheerfully, "Just doing your windows."

Patience was flabbergasted. In a rage, she flew downstairs and out the front door.

"What the hell are you doing? Get down immediately or I'll dial 911."

"That's alright, " said Mike genially, "I've finished anyway. You just need to pay."

"Pay? You've got to be frigging joking!"

"I'm sorry. But a job's a job."

By this time, curtains had started to twitch. Patience was suddenly aware that she was on show and, seeing as she had yet to apply make-up, she was not quite the 'sight' she intended to be.

"Alright then. How much? Miguel! Get out here!" yelled Patience furiously.

"Thank you kindly, miss. Two please."

"Two pounds?"

"No. Two hundred pounds. It's Ascot week. Special rates apply," said Mike apologetically.

Miguel appeared, clad only in a pair of CK boxers, and handed over the money. Patience stormed back into the house. Next door, Angela and Pete watched the whole affair through the window. In their opinion, Round Two had definitely gone to them.

Over the course of the next two days, Patience was forced to give several designer dresses for a jumble sale, make a major donation to the Scout jamboree, the meters were read three times and her boiler was serviced twice. An unsolicited order of twenty pizzas was delivered and, since Patience was only allowed an impossibly small number of calories each day by her dietician, this was infuriating on many different levels. All of this was causing tensions between her and Dack, particularly since Patience had put their sex-life on hold on account of all the stress.

On the third Race Day, Patience was not enjoying the racing one little bit. She had failed to pick out a single winner and Miguel and Dack had both disappeared, leaving her with a crowd of extremely snooty aristocrats who thought America should have remained a colony. She left the stadium to go home and have a long soak in the rather small bath. On the way back, she thought about how she could put a stop to the rather childish pranks being perpetrated by the neighbours. She was not a Hollywood diva for nothing and knew how to wield power when she wanted to. She couldn't decide whether to flatter their egos by an appearance or threaten to sue the pants off them.

She knocked on Angela and Pete's front door and was greeted by shocked surprise on their faces.

"Oh! We thought you were at home already!" said Angela.

"Aren't you going to let me in? I think we have things to talk about, don't you?" said Patience, pushing past them into their front-room.

"Now," she continued, "I know what you've been up to and…"

Patience's sentence petered out as she became aware of the sound of a couple having sex extremely loudly carrying through the terraced walls. One of the participants was very obviously Dack, judging by the frequent cries of "Oh Baby", in an American accent.

"But if it's not you, then who is it?" asked Angela, aghast.

A woman's voice was then heard saying, "By heck! That's blooming marvellous."

Pete gasped: "That's Sharon Stubbs from number 37. You can hear her halfway down the street, when she gets going."

For Patience, this was the last straw. She resorted to the most effective weapon in the diva's armoury – she burst into tears. Angela for her part did what was natural in a crisis situation. She put the kettle on.

That evening Patience eschewed the company of the 'A' list brigade in favour of an evening down the Knavesmire pub with her new friends, Pete and Angela. Patience was still feeling somewhat vulnerable and it was important to her that she had people around her. It didn't matter who they actually were. She imagined herself in the role of Blanche in 'A Streetcar named Desire' – dependent on the kindness of strangers. Besides, she had been flattered by how they rallied to her support during this traumatic time and decided that she could forgive them for their earlier indiscretions. She liked to think that she was still in touch with her fans – just as long as she didn't need to meet them too often.

Following Dack's latest relapse from his sex addiction recovery programme, Patience had thrown him out of the house. He was on his way to London in a taxi in search of a hotel with vacancies – preferably not too far from a singles' bar. Miguel was temporarily in hiding, knowing that his best strategy for survival was to lie low for the night. Never one to miss an opportunity, he was currently getting better acquainted with the rather attractive daughter of Lord someone-or-other.

In the pub, the beers were flowing and tongues were being loosened. A large crowd of the neighbours had joined them, but Patience was finding the slightly rowdy, but nonetheless honest, chat round the table rather liberating.

"Anyway, as I said to the bishop, your mitre is simply not going to fit in there…"

The crowd around the table chuckled appreciatively at

Patience's story. Now that they had got used to having a movie star in their midst, no one was quite sure what all the fuss had been about. She was quite ordinary really – burped and farted just like everyone else. Probably.

It wasn't even as if she was the biggest star round the table. They all turned from Patience and listened with rapt attention as Richard Whitely put down his beer and began to recount another tale of behind the scenes of 'Countdown'. Everyone agreed that there was a real star – from Yorkshire and everything.

The Prologue in Modern English

Here Begins the Book of the Tales of York

In every season in York's faire city

Pilgrims come desiring sights to see;

The Minster, castle, walls and dungeon, too,

And look for good times all the city through.

They walk the way of Constantine of Rome,

The Vikings, priests and knights – and then go home.

But though York is a town of such beauty

The stones and streets do not make a city.

For in these streets there men and women throng

Who live and work here through the whole year long.

The heart and voice these people are indeed

Of this city. I swear, so Christ me speed,

That throughout the world you may never see

So noble or so merry a company!

The farmer, the beggar, the student, the wife, the cook

And many more will you find here in this book;

The high and the low, hard workers and a right shower,

Al grow together and here are the flowers

Of their experience and learning, both earthy and sublime.

So quieten down and join me for a time

For, as in Chaucer's tales of Canterbury,

So now in the tales of York, as all can see,

Will folk set forth their wisdom and their jest,

And I will set them down, or do my best.

From old cities come new stories, surely,

All kinds of tales are told and written, truly.

Now, that's me finished, there is no more to say.

Our tales begin; we must be on our way.

The Quotes from Chaucer in Modern English

The Beggar's Tale

"He was the best beggar..."

The General Prologue (line 252)

The Story-Teller's Tale

"But yet I pray of all this company
That if I speak from my own phantasy,
They will not take amiss the things I say;
For my intention's only but to play."

The Wife of Bath's Prologue (lines 189–192)

The Carriage Worker's Tale

"To church my man was borne upon the morrow
By neighbours, who for him made signs
of sorrow..."

The Wife of Bath's Prologue (lines 593–594)

The Graduate's Tale

"That I'm quite drunk, I know it by my sound:
And therefore, if I slander or mis-say,
Blame it on ale of Southwark, so I pray..."

The Miller's Prologue (lines 3138–3140)

The Tale of Fred and Ginger

"Fresher and jollier in his array,
In my opinion, than the month of May.
He sang and danced better than any man
There is or has been since the world began."

The Franklin's Tale (lines 315–318)

The Farmer's Tale

"As when a man has been in poor estate
And he climbs up and waxes fortunate,
And there abides in all prosperity.
Such things are gladsome, as it seems to me,
And of such things it would be good to tell."

The Nun's Priest's Prologue (lines 2775–2779)

A Tale of Two Sisters

"After pride I will speak of the foul sin
of envy, which is, according to the word
of the philosopher,
sorrow for other men's prosperity..."

The Parson's Tale (lines 484–486)

The Old Wife's Tale

"A husband must not be inquisitive
Of God, nor of his wife, while she's alive.
So long as he may find God's plenty there,
For all the rest he need not greatly care."

The Miller's Prologue (lines 3163–3166)

The Trainer's Tale

"A man must needs have love..."

The Knight's Tale (line 311)

A Very Blue Tale

"And therefore to all men this tale I tell,
Let gain who may, for everything's to sell.
With empty hand men may no falcons lure;
For profit would I all his lust endure..."

The Wife of Bath's Tale (lines 413–416)

The Mature Student's Tale

"Yet pray I all who read what I do write,
Forgive me that I do no diligence
By subtle change to make the story right..."

The Second Nun's Tale (lines 78–80)

Leonard's Tale

"You lie here, full of anger and of ire,
Wherewith the Devil set your heart afire..."

The Summoner's Tale (lines 273–274)

The G.P.'s Tale

"The foolish husband, always he must pay..."

The Shipman's Tale (line 11)

The Student's Tale

"Heard I of a miller better brought to mark.
A wicked jest was played him in the dark."

The Cook's Prologue (lines 4337–4338)

A Child's Tale

"A pleasant tale in prose I will relate..."

The Parson's Prologue (line 46)

The Tale of Griselda and the Chair

"This story's told here, not that all wives should
Follow Griselda in humility,
For this would be unbearable, though they would,
But just that everyone, in his degree,
Should be as constant in adversity."

The Clerk's Tale (lines 1096–1100)

The Cook's Tale

"He was as full of love, I may aver,
As is a beehive full of honey sweet;
Well for the wench that with him chanced to meet."

The Cook's Tale (lines 8–10)

A Poor Man's Tale

"Amongst these humble folk there dwelt a man
Who was considered poorest of them all."

The Clerk's Tale (lines 150–151)

The Clerk's Tale

"Look out a thing we may not lightly have,
And after that we'll cry all day and crave.
Forbid a thing, and that thing covet we;
Press hard upon us, then we turn and flee."

The Wife of Bath's Prologue (lines 517–520)

The Actress's Tale

"For par amour I loved her first, you know.
What can you say? You know not, even now,
Whether she is a woman or goddess!"

The Knight's Tale (lines 296–298)

Author Biographies

Rosie Canning

Rosie lives in North London. She recently completed an MA in Creative Writing at Middlesex University, where she sometimes works in the library. She is finishing her first novel *The Stolen Child*.

Matt Charnock

Matt moved to York after graduating from Ripon and York St John College, where he studied Drama. Since graduating, he has been creating his own unique brand of street theatre, entertaining the tourists and citizens of York. He loves cheesecake, coffee and his wife. Matt also tries to play squash.

Maggie Cobbett

Born and brought up in Yorkshire, Maggie daringly crossed the Pennines to study in Manchester. After years of alternating between teaching Modern Languages to the British and English to the rest of the globe, she is deriving new inspiration for her writing from work as a TV/film extra.

David Darton

David is part-time strategy director of the Equal Opportunities Commission and a freelance business consultant and writer. Most recently, he edited *The Right Use of Money* for Friends Provident. David lives with his partner, Colin, and shares care of his three children. He lives in York and is writing a thriller.

Imogen Featherstone

Imogen works as an occupational therapist in York. She previously completed an English degree and has continued to follow her interest in creative writing since then. She enjoys writing short stories and has had several articles published in magazines.

Rachael Forsyth

Born in North Yorkshire, Rachael is currently studying Music at Middlesex University. Now in her final year, she is preparing to begin her career as a professional saxophonist. She has always had a passion for writing and has just completed her first novel.

Maxine Gordon

Maxine was born in Edinburgh in 1968 and has lived in York since 1997. She works part-time as a journalist at the *Evening Press* and is married with one daughter.

Sam Haward

Sam was born and grew up in Yorkshire. He studied Plant Sciences at Queens' College, Cambridge, where he complete a PhD. He has since joined the National Health Service, working as a primary care manager. He has spent time travelling and worked on a kibbutz before University.

Gwyneth Highley

Gwyneth recently fulfilled a lifelong ambition when she gained a BA in English Literature from York St John College. As part of her course, she chose to study creative writing, but only as an alternative to the even more dreadful prospect of studying IT. Gwyneth intends to do an MA in Creative Writing.

Andrew Jenkinson

At the age of 61, Andrew has spent most of his working life within the agricultural industry on the technical, advisory and selling sectors. During his younger days, he had a yokel comedy act, appearing in shows and cabaret in Norfolk. Married with one daughter, he enjoys the countryside, theatre, reading and comic writing.

Ryan de Koning

Twenty seven years old, Ryan studies English and Creative Writing at York St John College. He also works in a bookshop in York. In his spare time, he enjoys walking and looking at clouds.

Linda Murphy

Born in Acomb, near York, Linda lived in South America before settling in Lincoln. After working for a local newspaper and writing and recording short stories for a magazine for the blind, she is now busily working on her first novels – her family saga set in York and a psychological thriller set in Cornwall.

Annette Oliver

Annette inhabits that shadowy world that lies between the City of York and the pure rural idyll that surrounds it. Her inspiration comes from many years spent people-watching and listening. For her, the Yorkshire idiom "There's nowt so queer as folk!" seems to grow truer by the day.

Polly Redman

Polly has developed her communication skills and imagination while juggling the roles of practising nurse, wife, mother, and student of English & Drama at York St John College. Writing, which had been an entertaining and therapeutic pastime, has now moved on to being an outlet for her expressiveness.

Helen Sant

Helen has enjoyed writing and imagining stories for a long time. She is currently a mature student at York St John College, undertaking a degree in Performing Arts and English. She also works as a tour guide/storyteller on her ghost walk 'Phantom Footsteps'.

Ian Stuart

Ian is an ex-teacher turned writer/performer. He is a founding student of the University of York and has stories accepted by the BBC and various local publications.

James Walker

James is the proud father of Billy and partner of Suzie. He is currently in postgraduate study. In his free time he enjoys reading, writing and menial part-time employment. If you would like more details of his writing, then please visit www.jameswalker.com.

Anthony Webster

Anthony was born in Acomb, York. From 1965 to 2000 he worked as a teacher, with some 'time off for good behaviour' in the 1970s to do research at Sheffield University. Since his 'retirement', he has had several part-time jobs, including teaching English as a foreign language, proofreading, church leadership, and freelance writing on education for the BBC.

Acknowledgements

Geoffrey Chaucer – *Canterbury Tales*
Everyman's Library, David Campbell Publishers Ltd, London, 1992.